MW01139841

Last Call with Jon Hobbes

By Justin Razza

For my parents

When I was 13 years old I was supposed to
give them my first paycheck.
I never did.
So I give them my first book instead.

"You can get much farther with a kind word and a gun
than you can with a kind word alone."

-Al Capone

"This country – right-or-wrong business is getting a little out-of-date…
History is moving pretty quickly these days
and the heroes and villains keep on changing parts."

-Ian Fleming

Prelude

A bullet whizzed by the brim of my fedora on the left side, obviously catching my attention. The next two fired at me were no less informative. I threw myself to the ground behind some crates and reached inside my coat for my own hand cannon to offer my own response, the trail of the bullets still ringing in my ears.

Only about half of the crates had been offloaded from the truck before someone decided to start this firefight. Luckily enough for me. A row of about twelve or fifteen boxes stacked three or four high were plenty for me to hide behind. I poked an eye through one of the slits between crate stacks to see if I had a clear shot at whomever was trying to kill me.

I didn't.

I shot blindly into the dark anyway, to give them something to think about.

It appeared they didn't have to think long, because I was immediately answered by a rain shower from a Tommy gun. To all the avail of a safety blanket hiding you from the boogeyman, I pulled my jacket up as close to my face as I could get it and tugged my fedora lower over my ears.

As the automatic machine gun still whirred, I thought of death. My own, specifically. I had always thought that death would be cold, but I was hot. Fire hot. And *wet*. That would be the blood. I was now lying in a pool of it. Strangely too though, I wasn't hurt. That's when I heard the soothing sound of running liquid and realized I hadn't been shot at all.

Slow as a turtle, I raised my head from under my hat to see the cause of the flowing rinse. The bullets from the Tommy gun had borne into the crates and broken some of the bottles inside. *Great*. Now they were leaking all over me.

I took the opportunity to reach up and break one of the boards of a crate that some bullets had already shattered and started for me. I pulled out the nearest unbroken bottle. Removing the cap, I had two thoughts.

One: I am going to take a healthy swig of this whiskey. *Cheap* whiskey at that. And if cheap whiskey is going to be the last thing I drink before I die, I am going to be *pissed*.

And two: Whiskey is *flammable*.

This time, not firing blindly, I put a bullet into one of the tires of the bootleg milk truck ensuring that it couldn't go anywhere. My only thought as I emptied the rest of my handgun into the gas tank of the truck, using it as an igniter for the whiskey to make the entire jalopy burst up in flames was *how the hell did I get here*?

The Long Goodbye

I was a cop.

Right up until 11:59 and 59 seconds on January 16th, 1920 when the Volstead Act took effect, ushering in Prohibition.

I didn't make that law and I don't believe in it. Nor was I consulted when it passed motion, or my vote would have been splashing whiskey into the faces of every member of the congressional board.

At five minutes til midnight I poured myself a generous tumbler of rye. Taking a gulp, I stared down at my contorted reflection in the brown, swirling liquid, as I set the glass down onto the bar a little too hard.

With a heavy sigh, I dropped a sugar cube into a flute. With a medicine dropper, I gave the tube a light squeeze and dropped three dashes of bitters onto the grainy white cube, staining it. I then poured champagne on top, completing the cocktail that everyone else in the room was imbibing to usher in this new era of forced sobriety.

I then made another for Betty, my buxom and dark haired cocktail waitress.

At exactly midnight, after a loud and boisterous ten second countdown as if it were New Years Eve, Betty and I clinked glasses. She downed half a glass of her bubbles in one sip. I purposely emptied mine on the floor, my private act of defiance for what I thought of this prohibition of alcohol in this grand country of ours, and went back to my brown water.

I was a cop.

Now I'm a bartender.

In literally one second, I flipped from one side of the law to the other.

Betty finished her champagne cocktail and blew me a cherry-red and breathless kiss and disappeared among the masses of the underground club to see if there were anything her patrons needed for continuance with their merriment.

Fifteen minutes ago I called *Last Call* for the final legal time in American History. But something told me now, as I stared through my glass out to the massive crowd of revelers in the room, that I would actually be *serving* Last Call tonight until sometime tomorrow.

I was a cop.

Now I'm a bartender.

My name is Jon Hobbes.

A Country, on the Rocks

It's been five years since last call on January 16th 1920. Five years since the start of a new sober era in United States history.

And none for the better.

The whole country is a Powder-keg, mob wars and gangland assaults in every major city across America. Chicago, New York, LA.

Even we here in Oldtowne are no exception.

Just as I predicted. That's why I turned in the badge. But *not* the gun. *Never* the gun. The badge was no longer a shield I could hide behind. But the gun, the gun was a useful and necessary tool for defense *and* offense.

I'm a bartender. With a gun. And a healthy appetite for the sauce. Deadly combinations. And those ingredients, combined with my knowledge of the law and my connections within it, plus my years of training are exactly why the Boss hired me. I'm a bartender sure, but I'm also a *bit* more than that. I utilize my contacts and my knowledge of the inner workings of the police force as a protector for our speakeasy. Occasionally the Boss has me go above and beyond the line of duty, but never above my pay grade (which is a *hell* of a lot higher than it was when I was a cop). Plus, I make a mean drink.

We call our saloon the *Ace of Clubs*. Because we're at the top, the pinnacle. Literally. We take the top three floors of the Boothby building downtown. Floor one is where I keep bar and we have the lounge and stage. Upstairs on the second floor is another bar and the casino. The top floor suite is off limits to everyone, as it's the Boss' domicile; he gets the Top. There's no card or club that can trump ours. We don't import cheap whiskey from Canada like they do in New York and Atlantic City. Nor do we resort to any bathtub Gin. We take the *big* risks, for the elite and exceedingly wealthy clientele. Champagne, cognac, Russian and Polish vodka, scotch. All named brands. Made properly in the proper regions from their proper countries. There are no skulls or XxX on any of the bottles behind *my* bar.

No sir, it's my job to make sure you enjoy a *proper* cocktail. So if you want a Sidecar or an Old Fashioned, a Gimlet or a French 75, a Bees Knees while you take in a crooner or a siren singing their souls out up on our performance stage, or a Ward 8 as you take to the tables in our casino, hell if you want a beautiful glass of a First Growth Bordeaux, I assure you I'll get it for you. At the *Ace of Clubs*, the customer always gets The Last Word.

So while the rest of the U.S. is falling to pieces thanks to a tyrannical government that has decreed that felling *good* is illegal, contrasting deliberately with some quote somewhere about the basics of Life, Liberty and the pursuit of *Happiness,* and federal forces uphold this unjust edict, the mob and gangs of every race, religion and creed struggle bloodily and violently to ascend the ladder of illicit substance control just so that Joe Everyman can get a well deserved drink after a long day of honest work.

What this country needs now is one big collective stiff drink to calm its nerves before the whole thing goes up in one big boom.

Bartenders, Broads and Martinis

The martini was stirred.

I poured the cool, clear liquid into the coupe for this Sensation before me. Her sparkling sapphire eyes never let her gaze break from me, not watching the cocktail slowly being poured nor when I peeled the lemon and dropped the twist into her glass. She was statuesque, as if her features were carved from a piece of marble that even Michelangelo would envy. Her face was angular and fierce, *seductive*, completely unlike the cute and cherubic face of my cocktail waitress Betty. No, this woman's was provocative and magnetic. A veil of blue-grey smoke from the cigarette she puffed through the long black holder, held in her elbow length black gloved hand only added to her allure and mystery.

She was everything a man could want. And desired.

That first sip of the gin moistened her cherry lips giving them a tantalizing sheen. And the seductive smile that played on her mouth promised more, just the more I was hoping for. Even now, as she took that second sip, she still hadn't even seen the cocktail, only knowing instinctively where it was, her gaze never leaving mine.

I started some small talk. *Where are you from? What do you do there?* And then the quip, *How'd you end up in a place like this?* We both laughed, knowing that my speakeasy was no ordinary one and that she must come from some place of wealth and power and privilege. And every minute move her body made, even from the smallest facial reactions and the way she drank and smoked and held herself, attested to this lifestyle.

The night was slow at the bar itself, but there were other customers to attend to and the girls who worked the room cocktailing needed to bring some libations out to their tables and into the gaming room for the gamblers. Banking on that telling smile of hers, I pulled away from the Sensation and her martini with the promise that I'd be back after I did some work. Her crystalline eyes followed me the length of the bar and she took another sip.

"I think I'll have some cognac," the Sensation told me when I returned before her and asked if she wanted another.

I cocked my eyebrow up in a sort of surprise. She returned the look.

"You disapprove," she questioned suspiciously.

"Not at all," I assured her. Actually I was impressed by her. I'm always impressed when a woman fancies the brown water. Especially one as gorgeous and exotic as this. "But don't you know the rule?" I asked her playfully.

She casually looked side to side about the room as if searching for some sign or plaque that posted the rules of the establishment. Her own delicate eyebrow raised this time, waiting for me to fill her in on the regulations we had here in the *Ace of Clubs*.

"I don't see any rules," she stated in mock protest, before I could begin. A casual shrug of her bare slender shoulders pushed her cleavage up momentarily for me to enjoy. This move wasn't an accident.

She went on, "And besides, even if there were, rules are made for breaking, aren't they?" A devilish smiled played across her lips. "Unless of course, they're *my* rules."

She leaned forward closer to the bar, again giving me a fine view of the tops of her breasts. (Still not an accident). And I had this funny feeling that she knew exactly where this conversation was leading.

"I still want some cognac," she demanded in a playful tone. "But even I can be persuaded to break my own rules," she added misbehavingly.

I put my elbows down on the bar and leaned closer to her as well. Only inches separated us. As with the martini before, without ever looking away from me she retrieved another cigarette from somewhere and fitted it into the long holder. Obviously, I lit it for her.

After a long drag, the red heat smoldering at the tip of her smoke, she asked casually and coolly, "What is this rule you speak of, barman?" Blowing the smoke in my direction. But the fire in her eyes, like the tip of her cigarette, betrayed her disinterested demeanor.

Of course I took her bait.

"The martini rule," I stated.

Elbow on the bar top the cigarette in her hand burning away unsmoked as she waited, she gave me a look that told me to continue.

"A martini," I informed the Sensation, "Is like a woman's breasts." Her attention was rapt now. "One isn't enough and three are too many."

Everyone knows that a woman can't resist a man in uniform, and as a cop I got more than my fair share of tail, but it's nothing like now. Even the uniform can't compete with this kind of power. Liquor does something to a woman. It rounds out their senses and dulls their inhibitions. Women are attracted to power and as a bartender you literally hold elixir bottles of that power in your hand.

Sleeping with beautiful women. It's a perk of the occupation.

The Sensation, of course, got her cognac. She was the kind of woman accustomed to getting her own way. But first, she had had that second martini; in accordance with the rules.

Now, my hand was sliding up the long gracefulness of her leg to her thigh. She *was* statuesque. Like a Roman goddess. And she was in my bed. Beneath me. Me, a mere mortal. She smelled like strawberries and scx and though her naked body was creamy white she radiated fire. She tasted like soft spices, the sweetness of the cognac still lingering on her tongue as my mouth found hers and my searching hand found something else.

The Sensation had a name, I found out the next morning.

Eve Tradere.

Last night we made love as strangers. When it happened again this morning we were... strangers, with names. Eve was insatiable. She really was a goddess. And I didn't need the third time we fell into it to prove it to me. She loved sex; I wasn't fool enough to think that it was just me, a mere mortal, a bartender. But a man can dream. Or at least feast on the forbidden fruits of the reward.

I enjoyed her willowy body greedily. And she used me as well. We lay glistening beneath the cool sheets for a long and dreamy coital morning. Eve's face was nestled lazily in my neck and I could feel her soft breath on my skin. I stirred when she slowly began to untangle our intertwined legs. Lifting her face to greet my own, the corner of her lips raised into a smile. They weren't as red as they were the night before, the lipstick long kissed off, but they were still full and luscious and I liked how they tasted on my own.

Nearly falling into each other once again as we kissed intoxicatingly, Eve pulled back and broke us apart.

"I have to go," she whispered.

In my disappointment, I moved in for another but she denied me. As she got up out of the bed I admired the nakedness of her lithe body, capturing in my memory banks the hourglass curve of her tummy, the rich fullness of the breasts that she flaunted teasingly at me last night, the way her ass moved as she walked. Gathering her clothes strewn about the floor, she began to dress. Her back to me so I could no longer see those lovely tits, she pulled on her undergarments. Before slipping her dress back on, still mostly naked, she cocked her head back to look at me and smiled.

That was fun, her eyes said, but no words were needed.

I got myself out of the bed as well, the scent of her still lingering in the air. I offered her a ride home, or wherever it was that she was going, but she refused. She would have a cab come around. And with that, Eve walked out my door and closed it softly behind her, no promise of future encounters only the lasting impression of a single night of spectacular sex.

Never Trust a Man with the Name of a City or a Color as a First Name

In this age of the absurd illegality of alcohol-induced merriment and drunkenness, security is paramount. In this, the *Ace of Clubs* was no different than every other speakeasy out there. While ours may not have been through a false door at the back of a butcher shop or delicatessen, we did require a password that changed nightly and only given out to a select list of preferred clientele in the upper echelons of certain social circles.

Guarding the door and collecting this nightly password, and even then having the authority to evaluate and allow entry or deny access with impunity, were the sharp eyes and large muscles of

Happy and Harry the Cat. The two bodyguards who stood sentinel at the door were charming, devilishly handsome, friendly, liked by just about everyone, myself included, cordial, gracious… and wouldn't hesitate to kill you if need be.

The Cat and Happy were deadly and dangerous. I preferred them at their station, guarding our saloon and my back. Either there or as my drinking partners. Much as I can hold my own in a fight, and even my training was probably better than theirs, I still would rather stay in their graces and on their good side.

But both men treated every guest who correctly gave the password and walked through our doors the utmost courtesy and respect. It was only when the occasional customer became unruly to the point of obnoxious obscenity that they were called upon to utilize their violent side. That is to say, they had to remove, albeit with force to set an example, that certain behaviors were not tolerated in our establishment. On the whole though, the guys were great. They watched out for the girls as they made their way around the room cocktailing, ensuring that they weren't harassed and felt safe. They blocked the doors from any unwanted riffraff and had their own inside track on sidestepping raids. And as I already said, they were fun drinking partners. In addition to these traits, there had been a few occasions over the years when on a particular missions that the Boss entrusted to me that they ended up being invaluable backup and sometimes saving my ass.

Harry the Cat sat on a stool by our inside door, chauffeur hat pulled down close over his eyes. We were at capacity and there would be no further admittance into the *Ace of Clubs* this evening.

So there was no need for either of the body guards to remain by the outside door to ask for the password for entry.

Happy was touring the room, his keen eye on the lookout for any infractions. While Harry was the more handsome of the pair, each of them got their equal fair share of attention from the cocktail girls working the floor. Tray in hand, en route to deliver some drinks to a table, one of the girls sidled up next to Happy, her face nestled by his neck and she whispered something into his ear that made him blush and she stalked off triumphantly. Directly he made his way to me at the bar.

"Gimme a bullet, Jon," he asked more than ordered.

In turn, I placed two glasses down on the bar and filled them with two fingers of a brownish amber liquid. We clinked the glasses together and downed the fuel. There was no way that I was going to let him take a bullet alone.

The waitress who made Happy blush returned to the bar for a fresh order for me to make. While waiting, she slipped close to Happy again. But this time he had a couple ounces of liquid courage in his system so he was ready and equipped for her wiles. I left them their own devices and privacy as I grabbed the bottles and proper ingredients to fulfill the order. As I was doing so, Harry the Cat approached the bar. Taking off his hat and running the fingers through his hair, he told me, "Hobbes. The Boss wants a word."

The summons was to be taken as a command. As soon as I finished what I was doing, I would need to take the secret staircase to the third floor to where the Boss called home and receive his orders and execute his bidding. I'm his bartender sure, but I'm also a bit *more* than that. Any one of the girls could hold their own in my absence. And besides, I knew he wouldn't keep me long. The Boss was a man who did not waste words or time. He was also a business man with a business to run. He wouldn't call me away in the middle of my shift if it weren't important. He would tell me what he wanted and I would be dismissed to carry out his wishes. Depending on the task, I would return to work out my shift behind the bar. Or not.

I finished shaking the Mary Pickford cocktail, named in the screen goddess' honor, and poured it into the coupe. After garnishing it with griottes, I was on my way up to the executive suite.

Making my way up to meet with the Boss, this would be the closest to a break as I was likely to receive all night. So while my mind should have been focused on the oncoming task I would be ordered to perform, it instead lapsed and I drifted back to last night with the Sensation. Eve. Her flirtatiousness, the way she smelled, the way she *tasted.* Her nakedness came urgently back into my memory and I savored her all over again in my mind. I wondered if I would ever see her again. Last night had been the first time she had ever stepped foot into the *Ace of Clubs*, I was sure of it. And there was no promise of a future engagement when she had left my company this morning. I was used to one night stands and I have peace (and pleasure) with them as they occurred frequently when I was still a cop and happened even more frequently now that I wasn't a cop.

But as much as I lacked in long term relationships, there had been a few women along the way who had been gracious enough to sleep with me more than once. These lingering effects from the Sensation had stayed with me all day and I wanted more of her. I wanted her to be more than a one time occurrence. I wanted to see her naked again. I wanted her beneath me again and succumb to me. Again.

I could almost smell her perfume as I reached the top echelon of the Boothby building, but it was snatched away from my recollection as I entered the Boss' sanctum. It hit me in the chest like a ton of bricks, the reality of my situation slamming into me as the effects of the Sensation recoiled immediately. It was time for work.

Floor to ceiling windows covered the long room, giving a three hundred and sixty degree panoramic view out over the night-lit city of Oldtowne. Lights from the other buildings and skyscrapers speckled in from the glittering world outside. The sight of the city from here was breathtaking. And it never got old, no matter how many times I had seen it from this very spot.

The room itself was grand and palatial. While I had come up from the *Ace of Clubs* via a secret stair that deposited me outside a moveable grandfather clock, off to my left was a private elevator for the Boss to get up and down from street level. Deep and plush black leather armchairs formed a sitting area at the start of the room off the elevator. Rich mahogany side tables held cigar humidors and crystalline bottles of brandy. Before me was a long, oak executive boardroom table. On the table was a snifter of brandy, already poured. This setup told me volumes. As only one snifter had been poured, I would be drinking alone. But nothing was new there. The Boss never sat with his underlings. In fact, I had never actually even seen the man in the flesh; he was a cautious and private man, keeping himself at a distance. The second thing I learned about the meeting ahead was what *wasn't* there. No cigar, no ash tray. With just the drink, I knew this meeting was going to be a short one and to the point.

I sat. I put my hand on the glass for something to do, but I wouldn't dare take a drink until acknowledged by the Boss. I waited.

But not for very long.

There was of course one more thing on the boardroom table, a mainstay fixture down at the far end. A speaker that fed into the room adjacent to this one, walled off by a two-way mirror where both the Boss on the other side of it could see me and I could see my reflection. The speaker was a marvel of our times and helped tremendously in meetings such as this. The system we had before was tedious, instructions from the Boss handwritten and sealed in an envelope passed through a slot in the wall. But two years ago some Australian* invented a two-way radio that was used in patrol cars. With contacts I still have within the police force, I was able to secure the technology and get a unit for myself. Now it's how the Boss speaks to me and any of his other underlings.

The speaker for the two-way crackled alive and the deep and masculine voice of an older man, the Boss, came through.

"Jon," he began. He always addressed me by my first name, never calling me by my last. "Warehouse 23. Down by the docks."

Ours may have been a two-way, but it was hardly ever used as such. It was definitely more *one* sided. That isn't to say though that our conversation only went one way. I can only imagine that the Boss was some expert lip reader or that he had some other means of hearing what I said besides the new radio, for whenever we conversed, even back in the old days of passing envelopes, he always responded appropriately to exactly what I was saying. Right now however, I said nothing and waited. The rustling of static intermingled with his voice, the Boss went on.

"At 4AM there is a boat coming in from France called *Sercial*. There are two crates on it that belong to me. Please go and retrieve them."

The Devil's Hour was cool and dark with a misty moon up above. There was a chill and distrust in the air, as there often was during this fell hour of the night. But I had all the warmth and security I needed packed in the holster beneath my coat. That's where I kept my hammerless Colt 1908 "Vest Pocket", the safety catch already disarmed. Just in case. Another "just in case" safety measure was my M1911 .45, my gun of choice, kept on my side. Both weapons are semi-automatic and I'm proficient with both of them. Just in case the devil, or any other adversary, decides to show up.

Absentmindedly my fingers brushed the .45 on my hip. I liked being reminded that it was there. As I waited, ignoring the dock workers as they scurried about their tasks, my hand reached inside my coat. The tips of my fingers grazed the metal I sought and pulled it out. The flask brimmed with whiskey that I kept in my coat pocket. I liked knowing that that was there too. Unscrewing the cap, I took a long drag and stared out over the harbor.

The night starless and the moon obscured by cloud, it was hard to tell where the sky ended and the ocean began. In the swirling violet that was the seawater, the *Sercial* came slowly out of the dark like a ghost ship through the fog. I took another sip of the fire-water in my flask and prepared myself to go to work.

The job the Boss set me on tonight was an easy one. Of all the cargo on the *Sercial* from overseas, only two crates belonged to the Boss and all I had to do was collect them and bring them back to his sanctum. What was in the crates? It isn't my place to ask. That he sent me to get them, they were clearly something of some importance. But as jobs go that the Boss assigns me, this was a dalliance.

The salt and seaweed in the air stung my nose. I wanted another drink, but the flask was back hidden in my jacket and it was time to go to work. Waiting stoically as the assembled crew of workers prepared for the arrival of the coming cargo ship and the captain brought her in slowly, the men ignored me and asked no questions. And I provided no answers. As far as I was concerned, they weren't even there and for them neither was I. Plausible deniability.

The only Bill of Lading I had was the whispered word I gave to the dock master. "Invisible" though I may have been, the unloading of my particular freight was suddenly upgraded with a certain degree of priority. Which suited everyone. They wanted me gone just as much as I wanted to be. The sooner this was over with, the less danger would we all be in and the smaller chance that we would get caught.

A hand-truck laden with my charge was carefully walked down the gangway of the *Sercial*. Two wooden cases stacked one on top of the other slowly made their way towards me. Wooden crates, with dimensions such as they had, and from France meant that they contained only one thing.

Wine.

Of course it could have been cognac too, but cognac crates tended to be a bit longer than these. And besides, when we received our shipment of cognac it was in significantly larger quantities than this.

The hand-truck was about halfway down the plank from the boat to the shore when I could just start to make out the markings etched into the boxes from the faint and hazy light of the pier.

That's when the first bullet whizzed by.

*Frederick William Donnie, an Australian policeman, invented the first two-way radio in 1923

The Count of Romanée

Fuck.

Was my first thought. *So much for being easy,* was my second.

Instinctively I reached into my jacket and retrieved my "Vest Pocket" and began firing back. The bullets were hailing from off to my left and I shot in the dark in their general vicinity. The dock workers ducked for cover and scattered like ants away from the fray. Me? I advanced toward the danger still firing.

In the heat of the melee, the man who was escorting the hand-truck with my quarry let it go to save his own skin as he dove into the black water to get away from the violence of bullets coming our way. Still shooting, I saw from the corner of my eye the hand-truck rushing out of control down the remainder of the gangway as it was let go.

Fuck, again.

I didn't have time to stop it *and* keep firing for cover to retrieve it at the same time. I was just far enough away to not be able to make a go for it, having moved closer to the gunman, or should I say the two of them I now calculated. Thankfully, the hand-truck had been far enough down the walkway to avoid going over the side and into the water. I could only hope it would come safely to a halt on its own.

Concerned more with my own life than the contents of the crates, I shot, reloaded, and kept shooting more rapidly now and mercilessly. There was a grunt of pain followed a moment later by a sickening thud as one of my bullets finally hit home on one of my assailants and he fell dead from his elevated position.

Angry bullets were returned my way, but I kept on, getting closer. It was either him or me at this point, and I was determined that it wouldn't be me. I still couldn't see him in the darkness, but I had his general location. I was an easier target on the ground, but the unexpected death of his companion and the fear that must now be ripping through him because I was getting closer unnerved him. I had seen it a hundred times back when I was a cop. He may have had the advantage, better vantage point being elevated and me not being as concealed in the shadows as he was, but the circumstances unnerved him. And I used that faltering to my advantage.

I slid another cartridge into the pistol and fired two shots. I was close because that's when I saw the darkness move. The whole world slowed down and went quiet then as I knew I had him. Somewhere behind me there was the purr of an engine, the soft lapping of the wake splashing on the sea wall, and the drone of *Sercial* itself. But all this was put out of my mind as I took careful aim at where the shadow had danced and sent a bullet there. There was a scream of rage and I knew I had him. I put another bullet in the man. And then silence.

The altercation was over and I had won. The sound of the water was peaceful. Even the baritone hum from the ship sounded soothing. And the running of the engine was… *Running of an engine!?*

I spun on my heel and my stomach lurched. There was a car backed right up to where the hand-truck with my wine crates had landed. A man was there, one of the crates in his hands. He froze when he saw me and for a long instant we just locked eyes and glared at each other. The two men who had been firing from my left had only been a diversion to draw me away from the vehicle sneaking up on the cache from the other direction. When that *I got you* grin appeared on his face, my fury at having being deceived and falling for it kicked in and I shot at him. And missed.

Only one bullet left in this clip. And he took advantage of that by throwing both himself and the package in his arms into the back seat of the car. There was a roar as the sedan took off, the driver not even waiting for the thief in the backseat to close the door. I wasted my last bullet chasing the car, but I knew it would be futile. I kept pulling the trigger anyway, long past any sense.

My chest heaving in fury and frustration, I stood alone there in the darkness of the pier. Everyone was gone, the skirmish giving everyone a disappearing act. The hand-truck lay at my feet, the second crate still by it. At least the thieves only made it away with one and not both. I never saw the driver himself, but I was *very* well aware of the man who had dove into the backseat with my merchandise. At least I had that leg up on the situation. The Boss was going to be furious however, and I did not look forward to bearing that wrath. He was a man who insisted on hearing bad news immediately, so with a sigh I picked up the box and steeled myself to go straight back to the Boothby building.

It wasn't often that I failed in a mission.

Fuck.

The great expanse of the table lay between me and the Boss hidden in his private inner sanctum and I was glad of the distance. Defeat was an enormous weight that pressed me down in the chair, as far from the two-way mirror as I dared. It was an eternity of anxiousness and bile racing through my system waiting for the crackling of the radio and the Boss' voice to come through and to have to tell him of my failure at the docks.

I was hired for my professionalism. My ability to follow through and get the job done. There was a bitter taste in my mouth and I found it hard to swallow. This was going to be a conversation I would not relish. And the coming reprimand was going to be even less enjoyable.

A cigar I did not deserve was set on the table for me, along with a cutter, an ashtray and matches. An etched crystalline tumbler and a bottle of brandy were out for my enjoyment as well. A drink I was *certainly* going to need; calm the nerves and steel myself against the coming chastisement.

I poured myself two fingers of the sweet auburn liquid while waiting and downed it quickly, hoping that the act would go unnoticed. One wooden crate, rather than the two that were supposed to be there, rested on the tabletop as a tangible reminder of my failure in the mission. I lightly brushed my fingers against the wood of the wine box, etched with the words Romanée-Conti and the vintage numbers 1923. What any of that meant was lost on me, as I may be a connoisseur of a great many of the finer things in life, wine was not one of them. It was French, obviously, the cargo ship *Sercial* having arrived in port from France and verbiage on the crate was also clearly in that romantic language. What was *not* lost on me however, was that though wine collecting may not have been my thing personally, preferring hard liquor to feed my soul, I knew enough about the subject that there were plenty of folks out there who do collect wine and that the business of it was a major one on a global scale. Especially in these day in the United States. The Boss was one such collector, and had the contents of these boxes not been of great importance he would not have wasted his resources or my time in having me personally execute the operation and go and collect them for him.

A job which I failed.

"Jon," came the Boss' voice through the crackle, "There's only one crate next to you." It was a statement not a question, but his voice was calm and even. My instincts prickled and I shifted uncomfortably in my chair. There was no anger in his voice and somehow this was worse than what I expected. Disappointment is always worse than being reprimanded.

"Yes sir," my eyes downcast.

There was a pause over the static of the intercom, which probably didn't last as long as it felt, but was awful nonetheless.

And then finally, after too many heavy heart beats thudding in my chest came, "Jon," still calm and cool and even. "Pour yourself a drink." I obeyed and more went into my glass than I would have poured a customer had I been charging them.

"DRC," The Boss began as I took a healthy sip of the brandy. "Domaine Romanée-Conti."

I took another sip and sat back in the chair, my nerves relaxing some. Finally. One of the things I truly appreciated about the Boss was his openness and willingness to share. For a man whose face was hidden behind a two-way mirror and face I'd never seen anyway. And I'd only ever heard his voice through the radio and who was to say that he wasn't disguising his true voice with some mechanism? Who the Boss actually was didn't matter to me. What I appreciated was the fact that he would divulge information to keep me in the loop and help me to understand the gravity of certain situations. He believed, and I agreed, that knowledge was power. Even more powerful and important than his identity. I sat back and readied myself for a story.

Domaine Romanée-Conti. "In eastern France there is a thirty or so mile stretch of land called Burgundy," the Boss' voice cackled.

I was regaled with a tale of espionage and deceit. Of murder and manipulation. Of double and sometimes even triple crosses. A long history of monks and French royalty. Of Renaissance men and spies. Revolution. Napoleon. And a bitter bidding war between Madame de Pompadour, mistress of Louis XV, and her enemy, the suave and debonair, silver tongued, lover of wine and women, Louis François de Bourbon, the Prince of Conti.

What I learned as I slowly sipped my brandy, so that I would miss nothing of the story and my mind remain unclouded, was that this thirty mile stretch of France called Burgundy is the most prized (and therefore expensive) wine making earth in the world. The vineyards are esteemed and create some of the most beautiful and certainly most sought after and expensive wine on the planet. And within that small amount of land, some parcels were more prized above others. With Domaine Romanée-Conti at the undisputed pinnacle, the very tip of the mountain. Domaine Romanée-Conti, at the top, alone. And *great* as everything else is, there is Domaine Romanée-Conti and *then* everything else.

I was nearing the end of the mid section of my cigar as the Boss finished. Absentmindedly my fingers circled my brandy glass without picking it up. For a long moment I focused on the blue smoke emanating from the cigar. And then once I had the nerve, I looked at the single crate of precious wine and the blaring empty space that occupied my failed attempt at securing the second.

I don't fail often. And when I do I don't handle it well. When I first sluggishly dragged my feet into this room after my defeat at the docks, I felt awful. A knotted pain in my stomach and the weight of tons of bricks on my shoulders. I looked at the sole crate and I ran my fingers along the etched Romanée-Conti.

And now I felt worse.

I inhaled the enormous gravity of my failure and the money and *treasure* I had just cost the Boss. I held in the bitter smoke of the final third of my cigar, stinging the back of my throat as a personal chastisement, before exhaling a deep cloud of regret.

"Now tell me what happened," came the cracked voice over the intercom.

Nice Guys who Finish First

It was my turn to tell a tale. And I would tell it liked it happened, no bullshit. The Boss had a keen nose for it and I wasn't about to deceive him. Just the facts, as they say.

The hour was ungodly. So very close to dawn. By the time I had made it back to the Boothby building with the single box of Romanée-Conti I was exhausted from both the long night and the weight of my failure. Anger and disappointment in myself pumped like adrenaline through my veins, keeping me awake for the Boss' story of the history of Burgundy. I wondered then, does *he* sleep? What kept him up nights, especially this one? What lie behind that secret wall? Were there creature comforts of a home? A stove, a refrigerator, a *bed?* What women had been allowed access back there, fortunate enough to catch a glimpse of one of the grand secrets of the universe only to be taken down as another notch of prey on the Boss' belt?

The Boss was waiting for me to begin. And it was already so late. So I cast aside the thoughts of the Boss' horizontal dalliances.

As I replayed the evening's events at the dock over and over in my mind, the one detail that struck me the most was his eyes. The thieve's eyes. For that one instant when our sights locked and we were both held in an invisible and impenetrable beam of vision. There was a sort of kindred there, a connection between us. I knew him and he knew me and for that eternal second before any bullets would be able to fly or driver of the getaway vehicle spoiled any of our plans, we sized one another up, judging, measuring. A silent battle of wills, of equal measure, as we stared into each other's souls and demanded the weakness of the other. In that long heartbeat nothing else mattered. Not the dock workers or the crates of wine, not the rolling wake of the sea in the harbor or the drone of the *Sercial*. Just me against him. And those eyes would haunt me until I killed him.

This was the first time I had ever seen the man in the flesh, when he snatched the crate of Romanée-Conti and dove with it into the back of the black sedan as it peeled off. But I certainly knew him by reputation.

Nicholas Edward Gyetti.

Also known as Nick Gyetti. But most commonly called, by his friends, and most certainly his enemies, "Nice Guy" Eddie.

You had to respect the Italian hoods and their affinity for irony. Gyetti was anything but a nice guy. I had heard he once hung a man by the groin with a meat hook and left him to die in a freezer over a weekend just for not properly addressing the current broad he was banging. Another time he set explosives in some chicken farmers house and blew up his entire family for being late with his monthly "tithe." His notoriety for cruelty and violence was legendary in the underworld.

"Nice Guy" Eddie was a Capo, or Captain, in Enoch Johnson's regime out of Atlantic City. A Made Man.

Oldtowne was typically under the radar. By no means were we the equivalent of New York or LA, or Atlantic City, or especially Chicago. So what Eddie was doing here now, popping up in Oldtowne, and just to steal a couple of cases of wine, was a mystery.

I understood now the value and enormous worth of those cases and why the Boss had sent me to fetch them for him. They were a prize for him, an expensive trophy, a jewel in his private wine collection. On the flip side, it also made sense then to send a man like Eddie to go and steal them. But was it Johnson who sent Eddie after the crates or was Eddie acting of his own accord? Was Eddie a wine collector? Or was something more sinister going on? Was Atlantic City trying to move in on Oldtowne? Regardless of the reason, his presence in my city was disconcerting.

There was silence beyond the wall, as I concluded my tale. My cigar was long stubbed out and I pondered my reflection in the amber liquid in my glass, waiting.

"Nick Gyetti is of little consequence," the Boss' voice crackled finally.

The Cat's Meow

I hit a hash house on my way home from the Boothby building, a cheap little 24-hour diner along my way that served perfectly runny eggs with the sun of dawn staring up, super crisp bacon and always a fresh pot of joe in the percolator. Behind the counter in the kitchen was the same grisly cook, big greasy arms bulging from a stained white shirt, consistently ringing the bell when an order was up. And like some Pavlov dog, a pretty waitress would scurry over to collect and deliver. He must be back there twenty four hours a day, seven days a week. When did he sleep? As the owner of this joint, it seemed he had more in common with the Boss than I did.

A pallid gold came in through the diner window, gaining in strength and heat the more it fought and vanquished the navy blue of the sky. Stars disappeared one by one, as if falling out of existence. Until finally it was just a battle of wills between the moon and the sun. Eventually the moon lost the battle, but I had a feeling it would be back tonight to reclaim its right as crown of the sky. Sipping my coffee I watched the dawn break into full morning.

My plate arrived, I could smell the bacon seconds before it was set down in front of me. It was dropped off by… I didn't catch her name. They were all the same, the waitresses here, pretty things in bloomers and fishnets. A little hat and a big red lipstick smile. Hair either pulled back in a bun or cascading down across both shoulders. Receipt pad in either hand or apron. I thanked the dame and then concentrated on my plate.

I ate ravenously. Good day or bad, win or lose, success or failure; no matter what, a man's gotta eat. In a caddy by the end of the table, pressed up against the wall, were shakers of salt and pepper, both of which I used generously. A crusty ramekin piled with sugar cubes that I left untouched. And a squeeze bottle of ketchup for those miscreants who liked to squirt it all over their home fries, or the worse sin yet, on their eggs. There were those who argued of course that a potato is a potato and putting ketchup on them was natural. French fries and ketchup go hand in hand of course, so why should hash browns and home fries get left out? I don't know, maybe I'm the crazy one.

This is the kind of shit that goes through my famished, delirious mind after a long bad night at work.

Dipping my toast and soaking up the translucent runny liquid from the eggs as well as the yolk, I stuffed half the slice of bread in my mouth in one bite and chased it with some bacon. My coffee cup never saw the bottom, as, … I didn't catch any of their names…, kept my mug full, a refill on every pass by.

Nick Gyetti is of little consequence, the Boss had stated. I was too tired to focus on work, but it certainly was a better choice of thought than the do's and don'ts of ketchup. He didn't mean it as an insult, saying that Eddie was a trifle of a man and someone who needn't be reckoned with. "Nice Guy" Eddie was a Made guy and was certainly a main player. What the Boss had meant was that his presence in Oldtowne was of little matter. If he was stealing the wine for himself or someone else, so be it. There would be no way to sell it on the Black Market. Romanée-Conti would only appeal to a very limited clientele given it's exorbitant price tag, even with the dry spell running rampant in the United States. And in that small circle of people who could have afforded it, that information would most certainly come back our way.

That being said, we weren't going to sit idly by and let this infraction pass either. I had very specific instructions. A reminder of who's territory Oldtowne was was a necessity, but we weren't about to start a full on war with other cities or their organizations. If sometime within the next twenty four hours, if "Nice Guy" Eddie raised his head and surfaced in Oldtowne, I was to kill him. If I could find out where he took the wine first and retrieve it, all the better. After those twenty four hours, however, taking him out was off limits. Unless of course a firefight started between he and I naturally, then may the best man win and I had the Boss' blessing.

As a last resort, I would go to Atlantic City, meet with Enoch Johnson in a conference that the Boss himself would set up, and we would discuss as rational men what kind of penalty would need to occur. Someone would die then, but it wouldn't be Eddie. Probably someone of a lower stature on the power ladder.

Hoping it wouldn't come to a trip to Jersey for a formal sit down with Johnson, our plan if after the next day ended and Eddie was still alive, we would simply hit them back. While every city was their own isolated world of underground booze and corruption, we all still lived in one big country. And across that expanse of land that I love from sea to shining sea, we all needed to cross borders and get our booze around. Decreed by Chicago and ratified by the rest of the country, a small tax was paid to the local boss of each city for every truck that came through, an agreed upon number that everyone paid. More out of principle than anything else and a small manner of keeping peace. Atlantic City had trucks coming through Oldtowne all the time. I was to simply knock one over. Nothing serious or even detrimental to Jersey's profits. One truck was small potatoes, an inconvenience, a fly in the ointment if you will. But it would be enough for our message to be heard. *Back off.*

This is what the Boss wanted. A message to be sent. Word would get back to Atlantic City, and after their own investigation into the transpiring events and discerning all that had happened, "Nice Guy" Eddie would be reprimanded by his own crew. The stolen wine was a minor slight against the Boss, not an outright attack on our territory or his business. So hitting one sole truck of Johnson's was small potatoes. Just hopefully without any ketchup.

I finally saw the stained bottom of my coffee mug, when my plate was cleaned of all breakfast items. The caffeine was just enough to get me home, my dogs barking and my bed calling my name. I couldn't wait to bury my face in the pillow and sleep this off.

Exhausted, I entered my building. It took everything I had to make it up to my floor, even with the luxury of an elevator and an attendant. I had been awake for almost an entire day, my breakfast had settled itself in my stomach and made me sleepy, and the adrenaline of last night's events had worn off and I was weighed down with the weariness of it all. My eyelids blinked slowly, stubbornly lifting again only because I willed them to.

And just when I had almost made it, when I was so close to home, only a hallway between me and my door, the hallucination began.

Against the wall, right by my door was an angel. A goddess in a tight midnight blue dress. Her long and lithe body leaning, one shoulder and one high heel balancing her. Long legs and short dress. Dirty blonde hair falling around her shoulders. And the smile of the devil on her face and the promise of sin in her sapphire eyes.

"Would you disapprove of some cognac?" She asked me with a wicked grin.

Next thing I know, before I could even comprehend what she had asked or who this seraph was, her white celestial hand was on my hip, grabbing hold half my pants and half my shirt and her tongue was in my mouth. It tasted of fire and her heat melted me into her. There was a distant taste of that cognac she had mentioned still lingering on her tastebuds and it awoke a fire within me as well. An angel? Perhaps I was wrong. More like she was the devil herself.

We were in my apartment then and our hands were everywhere. Our mouths locked together. Had I opened my door or had she? As if we were one body, I clumsily and lust-driven stumbled forward and she stumbled back. Her dress was off, tangling at her feet she struggled out of it and left it behind on the floor. Had I taken it off of her or had she? Out of it, she was completely naked from the waist up, and down there just out of my peripheral was something lacy, black and small. My wandering hands found her bare breasts and enjoyed their firmness in my hand. A nipple puckered and its stiffness brushed against the center of my palm. I had to have it in my mouth. Somehow, with eyes closed I found it and sucked greedily as she gave a moan of delight, her head falling back and her body going limp with a spasm of pleasure in my arms.

We fell onto my bed. Had I led us there or had she? I was delirious with lack of sleep. And lust. For this sensational creature, regardless of where she came from; the clouds above or the depths below.

Sensational.

That word struck a chord in my mind. She was *sensational.* The Sensation.

Her name was Eve.

She was ever impressive, this one. And when I ripped off my blazer and my pistol made a thud when it hit the floor, she kissed me harder, turned on that I had a gun rather than afraid. Instinctively my body reacted and matched her enthusiasm. My shirt *she* had torn off, of that much I was certain of at least; the first act I was sure one of us had done so far. Her fingers were at my belt then, deftly removing the obstacles in the way. My hands slid down either side of her body until I found that beginnings of that small black lace and removed her panties; her legs arching up to aid my endeavor. She was just as excited to have them off as I was.

Sometimes you think of the strangest things during sex. As I penetrated her, instead of focusing on her gasp of pleasure or even my own sensations of fervor and desire, as I entered her my thoughts went back to the dock. How the dark ocean night had enveloped me. How twelve bottles of the most expensive and seductive wine on the planet had disappeared in the mist. How the taste of brandy mixed with cigar smoke was bitter with disappointment rather than delectable.

A growing mount of rage began to storm through me as I started into her. The violence in my body took over our passion, like some form of inspiration. I buried my anger in her, taking it all out on her. My fury and outrage in every hard thrust. Her eyes were sealed shut, taking it all in. Her face squinting in pleasure and in pain, her body silently calling out to me for more. More. *More.*

There was something animalistic about our love making. Could I even call it that as her nails clawed shreds into my back, like some cat digging into its prey? It was a hard *fuck*; love had nothing to do with this. I used her and she used me. Both of us greedy, taking every ounce of pleasure the other would give. And then stealing some more.

We were all over the bed, unconsciously making sure that ever single space was utilized. She was here and I was there. I was one way and she another. The blankets a tangled knot beneath us, until we rid ourselves of them. Our sweating bodies keeping us warm enough. I'm pretty sure it was she who had thrown the blankets to floor, for she was on top of my right after, giving me a matching set of marks to the ones on my back, her nails slashing into my chest, as she took her pleasure. Taking advantage of her body as it racked and her head was thrown back, eyes firmly shut, I flipped her back on to the bed and took her as she had just taken me.

It took only seconds but felt an eternity of bliss. She pulled me closer into her as I finished, not wanting to stop, not wanting to let go, to be as much a part of this as she could. To stay as one.

Heaving, one final spasm rippled through me. Her breath felt hot against my neck and she kissed the lower part of my ear, bringing the soft lobe into her mouth for a gentle suck. Heart thundering in my chest, I tried to find her mouth as I steadied my breathing. I found her jaw and kissed it. And then jaw again, but closer to the chin this time. Her mouth was searching for mine now as well and my lips met her cheek. And then finally, we found each other and we kissed.

Slowly.

Slower.

Slower still.

Until the night finally ended and we fell asleep.

Pillow Talk and Concrete Boots

Before I even opened my eyes, I could smell her. The tang of lingering perfume, pheromones and sex. Eve was still in my bed. Next to me. I could feel her naked skin against mine and an electric current went through my body. Shifting my legs to feel more of hers and the stiffness a man feels in the morning when he wakes up turned into something else.

Opening my eyes, I turned to get a better look at her sleeping form. At some point during our slumber one of us must have retrieved the blankets from the floor. Even still, we hardly used them and were barely covered. The majority of her nakedness was exposed, causing a stir in the lower half of my body. It was like I could literally feel the flow of hot blood coursing through me. I watched her slow, steady breathing making her breasts rise and fall, enjoying the view. Her tits were perfect, gravity and age not yet beginning to take its toll, still firm so that with each breath they moved straight up, her blush pink nipples like a beacon reaching for the stars.

The rest of her slender body was no less magnificent, *sensational*. I dared not touch her, for fear of disturbing her, though I longed to. Desire was fighting to take over me, but I held it at bay. The inlay of her bellybutton a tantalizing whirlpool vortex in the flat ocean of her stomach. Even more so than her breasts, the sexiness of her stomach aroused me more and it was gazing at this that I nearly lost control of myself and ravaged her while she still slept.

"It's impolite to stare," she chided, letting me know she was awake. There was a mischievous grin curled on her face as I looked into her sea blue eyes. "Unless of course you intend on doing something about it."

I was on top of her then and we were kissing. The breasts that were moving rhythmically moments before were now crushed beneath me. Our legs played together for a moment, until I pried hers apart with my own.

We made love again. With less ferocity than the night before but no less fervor.

"Have you ever killed a man?" Elbow propped up on the pillow, Eve's eyes boring intently into me. She was referring, I know, to the gun she had heard hit the floor so much earlier this morning.

The day was wearing on, day-bright outside it had to be well past noon. Between our sleep and intermittent love making, the day was progressing. For me though, this day was starting off far better than how the last one turned out. A beautiful, naked woman lying by my side, readily giving herself to me. Those blue eyes and perfect tits for me to look at. Why had she come late last night, or early this morning, whichever it was? Was our sex the other night so good for her that she was greedy for more? Was she lonely and knew she would find a ready bedfellow in me? Truth is, I didn't care. She was here and looking at me. We enjoyed each other several more times over the course of the morning. When she had left my apartment the other night there was no telling if I would ever see her again. But with her waiting outside my door this morning, anxious to get her clothes off, it was probably the easiest sex I've ever gotten.

As she lay here now, though, a sheet was pulled up covering her nakedness. I was only allowed to see her face down to her clavicle and the upper beginning of her chest plate. Not even any cleavage was exposed. The sheet acting as a barrier between me and more of her sex.

Her lips turned up into a smile, waiting. "Well?"

"Yes," I told her, not breaking eye contact. For half a heartbeat I watched how that registered with her, to gage her reaction. "But only for food." I added jokingly.

She squealed a laugh and hit me with her pillow. I responded in kind with my own pillow, but her attack had made the sheet come loose from her and her breasts were on display for me to see once again. At the sight of them, the fight didn't last much longer as I whipped my pillow behind me and moved in on her. She succumbed easily and willingly and we wasted away more of the afternoon.

This however was the last time for the day, for when we were finished, she got up with a finality and told me she had to go. Where? To work? This woman had never had to work a day in her life; for all I didn't know about her, I was certain of that. She was just that type. Probably she had a long, liquid lunch engagement somewhere with the girls.

"Working tonight?" She asked as she slipped her dress back on.

Me, still in bed, watching her, already missing her nudity and she covered up, "I always work," I answered honestly.

She turned and walked to exit the bedroom door. Over her shoulder she said, "Maybe I'll pop in tonight for a drink."

"I never said I'd be working the bar tonight, I just said I'd be working," I told her playfully. "Maybe I'll have to kill a man."

Eve paused. Standing in the door frame of my bedroom, she turned her head back and gave me a wink.

I stayed in bed long after she had gone. Even past the point that I realized I was starving and wanted, needed, some lunch. But I reflected on all the events from last night until now, with special detail to everything from this morning.

In that short second that I internally recorded her response to me having killed someone before, remembering how she was even more hungry when she had heard the sound of the pistol thudding to the floor as we ripped our clothes off, I had seen that there was a cool calm there in the deep sea of her eyes. No fear. No shock. Eve Tradere, this goddess, this sensation, she was impressive indeed.

I returned to the scene of the crime.

It was time for the changing of the guard. I think.

All the waitresses here at the *Two Bits,* the 24-hour diner I ate breakfast at this morning all looked the same. I had a late lunch of steak and frites. Ketchup for the fries; but if that shit got near my steak, I'd kill you.

After the first cup of coffee did the trick, fueling my body with the caffeine strength to get me through the day, I started adding some Irish whiskey to the joe. This wasn't a service offered to very many customers, but there were a few of us who frequented the diner and were trustworthy enough to be in the know. The cook who never seemed to leave stored some hooch in squeeze bottles that he kept on the cooking line. Hidden right in plain sight, with handwritten labels of 'olive oil' or 'vinegar' and such. Of course, such a dangerous amenity came with a cost. The price of your meal would "mysteriously" go up. The plate of two eggs with bacon, sausage, toast and home fries went from 15 cents to seventy-five. My steak and frites rose from one dollar to two. While the dames here at the *Two Bits* didn't quite make it the way I would have, literally just adding whiskey to the black coffee, I didn't begrudge it. It also did the trick, performing as I needed it to.

My plate cleared and my third cup of coffee almost gone, I debated on a slice of the freshly baked cherry pie the waitress had offered me. The sweet aroma of sugared cherries had haunted we patrons of the diner throughout our meals, as the pies finished baking. In the end, I decided against it. The whiskey in my system was enough sugar for now. But I would be back for a piece later, though I knew it wouldn't be nearly as good after an afternoon of sitting out as opposed to straight out of the oven now. Leaving cash on the table, I tipped twenty percent on the bill and added an extra fin for the troubles.

True to my word, I went to work. On a day after a major screwup, it was better to go in early and show some humility than on time with acts of contrition.

Butterfingers Nelson.

That was the name I was charged to focus on today. Nice Guy Eddie to take a back seat; much to my chagrin. But who was I to argue or countermand the Boss? Especially today.

Butterfingers Nelson was a semi regular player with us in the *Ace of Clubs* casino. He had been playing poker on and off at our establishment for at least the past six months, maybe a shade longer. He had been invited into the knowledge of our sanctum and to a seat at the table by Ted Eastman, owner of the First Bank of Oldtowne. Eastman has been playing cards with us since the beginning, dropping all of his easily earned banking dollars, the marbled fat of the cash cow so to speak, to the *Ace of Clubs* and the other players of the game. He may have been brilliant in the financial world, but at our table he was easily one of the worst players I'd seen.

Butterfingers Nelson was one of his executives, not as rich as his boss in the banking circles but a better card player. He wasn't always knows as Butterfingers, actually today was the first time I had heard Nelson have an epitaph. He had received the moniker sometime between last night and now. After amounting a large number of the other player's chips, cigar smoke and animosity choking the room as Nelson was making a killing, he was caught during his deal pitching from the bottom of the deck.

He had always done fairly well for himself, but last night he was raking it all in. But who knew for how long he could have been cheating? There was an uproar of outrage upon him being caught. Gentlemanly conduct aside, the players had leapt from their chairs and the accuser flipped the table, sending cards and chips raining into a new game of fifty-two thousand dollar pickup.

Nelson had apparently bolted before most of the other gamblers were even up. And I was not behind the bar, already down at the docks to pick up a couple cases of wine. Given the lateness of the hour, the rest of the staff was more lax. Neither Harry the Cat or Happy were on the door, no longer a necessity for the evening. Happy, he said, was in the can at the time. And Harry was resting on his laurels flirting with the cocktail girls. He admitted this freely. Telling the truth to the Boss was always the best course of action and we all knew it. Regardless, Butterfingers Nelson, as he was now called due to his slippery fingers during his deal, had gotten away.

Apparently I wasn't the only one to have a bad night last night. I chanced a glance at the Cat and felt sorry for him. He was beating himself up over it as much as I was, you could see it all over his face.

That was two blows to the *Ace of Clubs* in one night. Not good odds. But at least one was more immediately rectifiable.

While Nice Guy Eddie was out there in the proverbial anywhere, there were avenues littered with breadcrumbs to find Butterfingers Nelson. The Boss set me on the hunt and dismissed me, leaving behind Happy and Harry the Cat with whatever chastisement awaited them.

As I slowly crept up the hallway, like some teenager sneaking back into the house, I took the gun from the inside holster of my jacket. Cautious and quiet, gun held with both hands, I advanced on Butterfingers Nelson's apartment door. The Boss was a clever man, a wary one and shrewd. With the forethought of a chess player who knows his next ten moves as well as his enemy's, he kept detailed files on every one of his regular and Big Time gamblers. For the high stakes games you had to be vouched for by one of the other players. Plus the *Ace of Clubs* was so exclusive that most of the clientele were rich and notable socialites; meaning it was easy to keep notes on the pedigree information such as names, addresses and birthdates. But it also made it simple to keep track of scandals they may have been involved in. And of course, it was the job of the cocktail waitresses at the *Club* to keep track and report who was sleeping with whom, outside of wedlock or otherwise, and report it. Regular logs and manifestos were kept of gambling winnings and losings. We kept track of what our clients liked to drink, how they took their coffee, how they liked to bet, and whether they preferred blondes or brunettes.

A full dossier with every piece of information we could use to serve you better at the *Ace of Clubs*. Or blackmail you later.

So of course we had Nelson's address. Did I think he was foolish enough to actually be here right now, being a wanted man and all? No, but I wanted to check it off my list. And as a rule, safety first. *My* safety. Hence the gun.

Approaching his door, I did one last glance around the corridor to ensure no one was there. I could kick the door in and take Nelson by surprise, provided he was even in there. But if last night's escape was any indication, Nelson was quick and I didn't want to give him any chance of getting away this time. I'd have to take the quiet approach and pick the lock. Years of being on the police force taught me this subtle art. There are all sorts of useful tools that you learn to keep on your person for a variety of situations. A ghost set of tension wrenches being one of them. Small and compact, fits easily in any of your pockets, and can get you into practically any door.

One hand on the pistol now, and with the other I insert the wrench and apply enough force to set the springs inside. With a click, the door opened before me. I'm quiet and open the door slowly. This is always the scariest part. The unknown. Not knowing what was on the other side of that door. Was someone in there? Were they hiding? Or were they waiting for you on the other side ready to blast you?

My heart thundered in my chest. I always hated this part. It's a very real fear, going through *any* door unwelcome and not knowing what awaited you on the other side. The door crept open, with each heartbeat I awaited a gunshot being fired at me. Finally, when none came, I was able to see full into the living room that the front door opened up to. All was quiet. Nelson could still be hiding though.

I searched room to room. It was becoming more and more obvious that Nelson wasn't here. But the place was disheveled, the bedroom especially. It looked as if someone had ransacked through the drawers and closet, packing a bag in some haste. So he had been here at least and was making an attempt to go into hiding.

Onto the next breadcrumb.

Butterfingers Nelson was a banker. What one thing would he need most of all to skip town and go on the lam? Money. And having been vouched for the game by Ted Eastman of First Bank, this was the next logical place to go. Nelson would have to go there, I just hoped I wasn't too late. I had wasted most of the day with Eve. And hopefully Eastman knew something.

The First Bank of Oldtowne was an ornate, stone structure. A throwback to Ancient Greek and Roman architecture. Large bricks of limestone made up the building, with an Ionic column on either side of the doorway. The entrance itself was crowned by a triangular pediment crosshead, with ground to ceiling curved arch windows to either side.

Inside was a business day as usual. Customers and tellers, the *ching* of money exchanging hands. Mid-level agents in their little glass cubicles assisting clients with loans. Administrators locked away in their posh offices behind closed doors. No guard was posted by the main door, I noticed, which was good. No one to interfere with me. On the far side of the airy hall was the massive and impenetrable vault door. Just before it was a spiral staircase leading to an upper floor, barred from the public by a green velour stanchion with chrome posts.

I made my way across the marble flooring, heading straight towards the spiral staircase. The good thing about banks, where discretion and privacy were paramount due to the handling of one's personal wealth, was that you were virtually ignored and left to go about your business until you, the customer, sought out whom you needed to speak to in order to conduct your affairs. I made it to the chartreuse barrier before anyone took any real notice of me. But by then it was too late. Without a guard to chase me down, the only obstruction in my way were the calls of halt from some of the agents who weren't busy assisting other customers.

I took off up the stairs to the floor of the executive offices. Warnings of *Stop!* and *I'll call the police!* still echoing behind me. Without an appointment, I moved down the corridor, plush carpet beneath my feet, to the suite of the Bank President.

I sat across the desk from Ted Eastman in his office, my gun between us. He didn't flinch. He didn't even look at it, his eye contact never breaking mine.

"You'll have to excuse me, Mr. Hobbes," Eastman began. I wasn't surprised he knew my name. He also wasn't surprised that I was there. "But this isn't the first time I've had a gun pointed at me."

"Where's Nelson?" I got straight to the point.

Eastman sat back in his swivel chair. Absentmindedly bringing the butt of his Cross pen into the corner of his mouth. He was reading the biography written in my facial characteristics and in my eyes, knowing me as well as anyone could. An ability, no doubt, that helped him ascend to the successes he made in his life.

By this time, one of those agents who was yelling that I wasn't allowed to come up here to this floor, was at the door to Eastman's office. I had locked it behind me when I entered however. Just as the pounding began, Eastman shot it down.

"It's fine, Johnson," Eastman called. "Mr. Hobbes has an appointment."

That was the last we heard from that fellow, Johnson, or anyone else who might disturb us. And then Eastman went back to sizing me up.

"Do you believe in luck, Mr. Hobbes?" He asked me, ignoring my question.

I wasn't going to let him get off so easily, however, nor play his game. He ignored my silence and pressed on.

"I do not," he told me. "But what I do believe in is *fortune*."

"Nelson?" I was getting irritated now. I didn't like my time being wasted and I'm not the most patient of men.

"It's men who lie, Mr. Hobbes," Eastman told me, as if I already didn't know. "Math, however, does not lie. Figures are a constant. I'm a numbers man." He steepled his fingers and peered at me as if he were unveiling great universal truths. "Numbers are cold, hard, *indifferent*."

Fucking bankers. What was this guy babbling on about?

"I did not achieve the status I have today by relying on Lady Luck. I amassed my fortune by believing in numbers. And adding zeroes before the decimal point."

If this guy didn't get to the point *soon, either before or after the decimal, I'd shoot him on principle for stringing me along. Nelson was out there somewhere and the longer I sat here the wider his gap of escape became.*

"I am an excellent card player, Mr. Hobbes."

That caught my attention. This guy is *terrible* at cards. He was always losing. I had just assumed that he was one of those old rich men who had nothing better to do with their money, one of those wealthy gambling addicts who no matter how much money they had in the bank, especially his own, it was never enough.

"Your Boss and I are business associates, Mr. Hobbes." Eastman informed me. This *was* news to me. "I lose money to the house because I help bankroll the *Ace of Clubs*. And I intentionally lose money to the other whales at the table to keep them on the hook so they keep coming back." He let that sink in. "The percentage of profits I earn from the *Club* far outweigh what I lose playing poker."

I shifted in my chair, taking this all in. My eyes focused on the pen lying on the desk that had previously been in Eastman's mouth. The pen. That was the weapon of the banker. It was on the desk before him, pointed at me, just as my gun was before me, pointed at him. That was our standoff. The Boss believed that knowledge was power and was therefore overly communicative, giving me all the information I needed and then some. I didn't like being caught off guard like this. I had no idea that banker Ted Eastman was a part of our organization. *That* was a golden nugget of information that the Boss had never shared.

"I assume you came here to question me on the whereabouts of Mr. Nelson." My eyes raised and were once again level with Eastman's. "You didn't actually think I was in on it with this man did you?" He smiled. And then he stood up, buttoning his suit jacket as he did so. "No, Mr. Hobbes, I was not aware that Mr. Nelson was cheating us. And like you, he also did not know that I have a stake in the *Ace of Clubs*."

As he began to come around his desk and leave his office, I picked up my gun and got up to follow him. Eastman stopped before he opened his office door to exit and he looked directly at me. Again that look on his face as if he were revealing great secrets of the universe.

"That is why he had no fear in coming here to retrieve his money. He probably assumed that because I always lost during the game that I would have a grudge of some kind against the *Ace of Clubs* and not care to see them cheated." Eastman smiled like the devil. "But once he was here, of course I would not allow him to leave."

He was here! Butterfingers Nelson right here in this ancient, stone building all along.

Eastman put his hand to the doorknob but still did not open the door, not allowing our secrets to leave the room. "I have him locked and guarded in the safety deposit box vault."

Butterfingers Nelson was sitting on the cold, marble floor, back against the hard steel of rows of safety deposit boxes. His jacket was off, carelessly cast aside on the floor and his tie was undone. He was pale and sweating. *Afraid.* Beside him was his lock box, filled with bound stacks of paper green. His entire worldly fortune, there was more money in that metal box than most people would ever see in their lifetime. But here, locked with him in this room, with no hope of getting away now, it was completely worthless.

An armed guard was posted as a sentinel outside the vault. So this is why there wasn't any security by the bank's main entrance. After he let me into the secured room, there was no longer a need for him to be here on guard duty. Eastman dispatched him to go get the armored truck they used to transport bundles of cash, hoards of five pound bags filled with bills and marked with a dollar sign. I was going to transport Nelson to… Eastman did not want to know where. His job done, he returned to his elevated office.

Nelson looked up at me and all the air went out of him. His body crumpled and he looked defeated. I held my gun loosely in my hand, hanging by my side. He couldn't take his eyes off it.

"You can come with me," I told him, "Or I can make you come with me."

By the flush of terror that flashed through his face, he got my implication that if I had to force him to come that the experience would not be a pleasant one. In desperation, he looked to all the money he had stored in his metal container. He wanted to buy his life. He didn't seem to realize that not everyone was motivated by money; this was always a foreign concept to people like him. Do I want to be rich? Of course. Do I like being paid, handsomely, for the jobs I execute? Naturally. What Nelson failed to understand was loyalty. That I was loyal to the man who was already paying me. And wether you could offer me more than him or not was irrelevant. Besides, Nelson cheated my organization. I despised that.

His money really was no good here.

"The easy way?" I asked him, giving him the opportunity to decide how he wanted this to go.

With a heavy sigh, he reluctantly started to get up. His life was forfeit and his body language looked it. But Nelson was a desperate man, and in one frantic last ditch attempt, he grabbed the heavy money box and flung it at me.

So, I realized, *The hard way.*

In the underworld, cheating was an unforgivable trespass. A sin that would not be absolved. Butterfingers Nelson was guilty of this transgression. As chastisement, I had his hands and feet bound with a high-test nylon cord, his unconscious form thrown in the cold, sealed back of the armored truck. I had assured Eastman that I would return the truck unscathed as soon as I was finished with… he didn't want to know. But I drove it with a very clear destination in mind.

As soon as Butterfingers Nelson had assaulted me with his cash box, he was at my mercy. His motion and the exertion of his throw was too grandiose and clumsy. His body was outstretched and vulnerable. Taking advantage of that was far too easy. The grip on the gun at my side tightened instinctively and I could have shot him then and there. But where was the fun in that? So I pistol whipped him in the head, rendering him unconscious. Then I bound him and tossed him into the back of the truck and locked him in.

My hunt for him had not lasted too long, and Nelson was fucked from the moment Eastman informed me that he was locked in the vault. I had given him the opportunity to come quietly and freely, which would have allowed him more dignity, but he had chosen otherwise when he tried to attack me. As his judge, jury and executioner I had decided that a bullet to the head and then disposing of the body was too good for him. He had cheated my organization and then attacked me. Sorry Nelson, but I had given you the option of the easy way. Now we were going to see Benny.

Benny was the kind of guy, whom years ago when I was still a cop, was the kind of guy we would routinely shake down. He wasn't an A List criminal, or even a B or C for that matter, but a small timer. A small timer who just happened to have his fingers on the pulse of the underworld of Oldtowne. He would offer up just enough information to keep himself out of jail.

Nowadays, it wasn't so much as role reversal as it was a partnership of sorts. He still provided me with information, albeit much more willingly now that we were on the same side of the law; that is, the wrong side. In return, I used what contacts and influence I still had within the police force to keep the heat off of him as much as possible. In addition to that, he's been added to the Boss' payroll for certain, shall we say, favors from time to time. And he would receive bonuses for his discretion and silence.

Benny was a gruff man, with a barrel for a chest, massive arms and a permanent five o'clock shadow. An Old Salt who told his tales with an impediment and only had one eye. He had lost it either in the War or a bar fight, depending on who you talked to. He was always shabbily dressed, a grease man ready to work on a boat or a car or some other *dirtier* work. And on his head was his staple, his trademark, his pride and joy, the ivy cap he had worn during his years in the navy.

He was already outside of his warehouse, poised half in and half out of an overhead light, waiting for me as I pulled up. Without a word, he nodded to me in greeting and then in typical Benny character, he did the grunt work of taking the limp body of Nelson out of the back of the truck and slinging him across his shoulder. At some point during being carried inside, Nelson came to. Naturally he struggled, but in Benny's strong arms he had no chance.

We went inside a broad concrete warehouse, the three of us. Benny was already prepared for us. He set Nelson harshly down in a chair, as if he were nothing more than a sack of product, his constrained feet in a basin. And then he walked away. Nelson's eyes were wide and pleading, staring at me.

"Please," he said. "Please," he repeated.

If he was attempting to petition my sense of kindness, he was sorely mistaken. We were all long past that point. Benny returned with a bucket and poured the contents into the basin that held Nelson's feet. Once emptied, Benny removed himself to get fetch another bucketful. I had to smile. Butterfingers Nelson however took a long, pregnant pause to comprehend what was being poured over his legs.

Liquid concrete.

The first bucket covered his feet to just above the ankles. The second would make it halfway up the calves, which would be more than plenty. We would wait until it hardened and then bring him out into the water. Still alive, we would drop him sinking into the bay. I could have killed him. I would have preferred to kill him. But I had given him the option. And this is what he chose.

Benny retuned with the second bucket.

Tails and Top Hats

"I killed a man today," I told Eve playfully.

She laughed, without a hint of nervousness, though unsure if I was kidding or not. And I made no attempt at giving away the truth of the matter. Her legs were intertwined with mine, sleek with the sweat of our love making.

After completing the task of Butterfingers Nelson, I returned to the *Ace of Clubs* and reported to the Boss, assuring him of a job well done. I was dismissed after giving him the details, to return to my station behind the bar. Towards the end of my shift, Eve came in for a drink and a fuck and when I had closed up we went back to my apartment together.

"And tomorrow?" She asked. "Are you going to kill someone else?" There were hints of both playfulness and seriousness in her tone. And she made no attempt at giving away the truth of her question.

I eyed her for a long moment. I liked this woman, though we knew so little about each other. The only thing we both knew for certainty was that we were sexually compatible. And despite her debutant ways, she was unafraid of the dangers I exuded.

"No," I answered seriously, after a time. "But I do have to hunt someone."

With the speed bump of Butterfingers Nelson behind me, I could begin my search for Nice Guy Eddie.

Eve was genuinely intrigued.

"Who?" She asked, the first trace of concern in her voice.

I wouldn't say his name, though she wouldn't have known it even if I had. "A man from Atlantic City." She was staring at me, a wavering in her eyes. "A Made Man from Enoch Johnson's outfit made a play here in Oldtowne the other night and I have to find him."

She clawed at my chest, both painful and pleasurable, and let slip the first crack in her tenacious façade, revealing a hint of her vulnerability. Smiling wickedly, I took advantage of this moment and took her again.

He had to be staying somewhere, Nice Guy Eddie. It's not as if Oldtowne was a skip, hop or even a jump outside Atlantic City; not just some day trip. Of course I had lost a day, so Eddie could be long gone by now. But my instincts told me differently. I may have failed, but so did Eddie. Like me, he only got half of the cache he was supposed to retrieve. So if my feeling was correct, he was still here in town. Had he been ordered not to leave until he had succeeded in securing both cases of DRC? Was he now scrambling to come up with a new plan to achieve the impossible and somehow penetrate the Boothby building, actually find where the Boss kept his hidden stash of wine (that even I didn't know), and then somehow break whatever security measures were set in place to get to it? And then of course there was the matter of escaping even if all that could be achieved. I thought that scenario very unlikely. My actual worry was that the initial wine theft was a precursor or even a diversion for something else. Either way, I felt it in my gut that Nice Guy Eddie was still here in Oldtowne.

And that meant that he had to be staying somewhere. Whether it was a ritzy hotel, a sleazy motel, or a pay-by-the-hour boardinghouse, in the city of Oldtowne the valets knew the comings and goings of everyone. Even if Eddie wasn't staying in any formal lodging, but crashing with an acquaintance or accomplice in some safe house somewhere, the valets would know. I never got a look at the driver of the getaway car down by the docks, but at least I could provide detailed information on Eddie himself and the car.

What did I know of Nice Guy Eddie besides the tales of his ferocity? Of whom he worked for? That information would not help me here. I needed an understanding of the man himself. What was his style? What were his appetites? Was he a man who reveled in the creature comforts that a man who raised himself to his position afforded him? Or was he still practical and someone who stuck to the roots he had come from, a hard man, a man who was comfortable going to the mattresses? Did he keep a different lady in each of the cities his business had him travel to? Or did he seek out the companionship of a lady of the streets?

Given that he had come here to steal the most prized liquid on the planet, whether for himself or someone else, I decided to start with the former. In my experience as a cop, I found that when most men who raised themselves up from a street level crook and became a Made Man, they got a taste for the Life and indulged in the luxuries that had been denied them their entire lives.

I started my search at The Empire, then the Boar's Tusks and then Congress. I got nothing from any of the three luxury hotels. Back when I was making my rounds as a cop, hotel valets and doorman were often utilized as a good source of information. Now that I was in my current business, they were essential. The men were dressed dominantly the same no matter the hotel you entered. Long black tailcoats with juxtaposed white gloved hands. Golden vests to match the epaulettes garnished upon each shoulder. Crisp oxford shirt, white to complement the gloves, and a black bow tie laced around the neck. And to crown the whole ensemble, a high black top hat. And because of this, and presumably given their "lowly" station in life, they went largely ignored. But they saw and heard everything. They put people in their cabs and knew their destinations and whom they were with. They were on a first name basis with every driver in the city. They saw every single person who passed through their revolving doors and entered the hotel. And whom they were staying with. When a politician brought in his mistress, they knew it. When a business man brought in his secretary for a "lunch break" they could tell you what kind of perfume she was wearing. And everyone paid for this intimate and invasive service; tipping these men in their serving uniforms and never even looking at their faces. Just top hats and tailcoats.

Each of the men who I inquired any information on Nice Guy Eddie from the first three spots were tipped handsomely and would contact me if they saw or heard anything. At the forth hotel, the Del Monte, I got a hit. Not on Eddie, but the car. It was here last night with its owner, and in a hushed tone I was told that he was allowed to indulge in the hotel's extracurricular activities. For the Del Monte, that meant he was allowed access into their casino. I had given each of the valets at the first three hotels a bigger tip than they would get from anyone all day, guaranteed. This doorman at the Del Monte received even more. And then I paid extra for his description, the vehicle owner, even though I knew it would be basically the same as every other low level thug who was only a getaway driver and hadn't yet made his bones.

"He came alone and left alone," the doorman informed me. "But he was drunk when he swerved his car away."

"What direction did he head?" I asked, though I knew it was no guarantee of where he may eventually end up. But at least it meant that Eddie was still in the city, or at least his driver was. My intuition told me that he was though and I took this as confirmation. Based on the direction that the driver had headed, there were two more high end luxury hotels up that way, the Starlight and the Dual Peaks. I decided to hit the twins first, as it was farther out and if that wasn't it I would double back to the Starlight and make my way back into my part of town and delve into the seedier parts of the city.

The Dual Peaks hotel took its name from its design. Not twin mountaintops, but rather east and west towers that rose mightily, an elegant lobby and great hall connecting them at the base. Your eyes couldn't help but look up the magnificent high rises, beckoning towards the sky. Several stories up, fifteen or twenty I surmised, a sky-bridge connected the two towers. It was indeed an impressive structure.

I pulled into the drive and under the porte-cochère. After striking out at the last several places, I didn't even bother getting out of the car. I was prepared for another rejection in my search and just wanted to move on to the Starlight and get back closer to the center of town. One of the guys came over and shook my hand, elbows resting on the door and his head inside my window.

"How are ya, Hobbes," he asked in greeting. "Heard you might be coming our way." Word in the valet circles travels fast, faster than I drive apparently, and I drive pretty fast. "What can I do for ya?"

First I gave the description of the getaway sedan and then its driver. I didn't even have to go any further. He lowered his head deeper into my car, closer to mine and whispered, "You're looking for Nice Guy Eddie." Nodding assent, clearly happy that he could help, he went on, "He's staying here. They both are."

All of a sudden I could feel the weight of the Colt 1908 against my body, awakening in it's holster inside my coat and my trigger finger began to itch. He was mine. At last. I just hoped that I wasn't too exposed out here beneath the coach gate and already given my position away.

"They're not here right now though," the valet dashed my hopes.

I scribbled a telephone number where I could be reached and wrapped the scrap paper around some cash in appreciation. And I wanted to be notified the second they returned to the hotel.

"That's a lot of spinach," the valet said, counting the tip with his eyes.

"And there'll be a lot more when I come back," I assured him.

I was feeling triumphant, as I steered back into the heart of Oldtowne. My foot pressed the gas harder with each jolt of elation. The roar of acceleration added to my sense of victory. I hadn't actually accomplished anything yet, per se, but at least I was hot on the right trail. And all of the doormen of the city would be more loyal to me and my wallet than to some outsider from another city. So the chances of Eddie finding out that I was *this close* on to him were pretty slim.

What I needed was to celebrate. I wanted a drink. And a steak. And then for dessert what I wanted was the *Sensation*. A bullet or two of bourbon, a rare piece of meat, followed by a piece of ass. Feed the soul, fill my stomach and then some tail. Yes, that is exactly what I needed now.

I stepped on the gas and went faster.

Dizzy with a Dame

I came from a three decker family growing up; my grandparents lived on the first floor, my family in the middle and my aunt alone on the top floor. And we were as poor as they came. That I fell into a blue collar life of a cop seemed only natural. The neighborhood I came from, people like us were destined to stay within the same rotating circle of social class, without escape. Even when Rosaline, my ex wife, and I got married, we moved into another triple decker home.

So now, even after five years, I still wasn't quite used to the Life. The High Life. But I was certainly getting better at it. The privileges and luxuries that my new employment afforded me were fleeting away from the foreign and I was becoming more accustomed. I went from banging broads in the back of my patrol car or in alleys behind diners to fancy hotel rooms. And the class of woman I found beneath me under five-star sheets also escalated in social quality.

Sitting here with Eve, the Sensation, in a restaurant like *Steve & Mildred's,* was something my mind would have never even been able to fathom once upon a time. And for our first date with clothes on, I was determined to impress her and show her a good time. The sapphire sparkle in her eye as she looked across the table at me told me she was thinking of a good time as well.

Steve & Mildred's was a place of juxtaposition. It was located at the pinnacle of a high end hotel in midtown. But despite being on the highest floor, giving the room the best view, it was a legit restaurant. Not like the *Ace of Clubs* or any of the dozens of speakeasies that covered the city. White table clothes were countered with black plate and flatware. Even the glasses were jet black. Clients on both sides of the law, provided they could afford it, dined here; judges, lawyers, mob bosses and capos, the chief of police. No alcohol was served.

Unless of course, you were one of the select few of Oldtowne who *Steve & Mildred's* could trust. Those folks could be served libations. Albeit discreetly. And nothing could be discerned through the opaque glasses.

The Boss was served alcohol when he dined here.

I was also given the opportunity.

Because of this entitlement, when the penguin attired waiter delivered the caviar I had ordered for Eve and I to start with, he also brought with him on his tray two chilled old fashioned glasses, icy steam rising off of them. Also on the tray were two carafes of a clear liquid and two shakers filled with ice.

"Would you care for some extra chilled water with your caviar, sir?" The waiter asked, making sure he could be heard by any watching and listening patrons. Since Prohibition began, this was an actual service that *Steve & Mildred's* provided. Extra cold water as part of caviar service, in lieu of vodka. Eve and I would not be receiving water however. Our ice coated tumblers would be filled with distilled Russian liquid. Vodka. A wonderful pairing with the pearls of black Beluga roe we were about to indulge in.

I nodded my assent and the waiter poured each carafe into a respective shaker. Then sealing them shut with a cover, he began to shake the cocktails, bruising the vodka as the liquid smashed against the ice cubes and reverberated against the inside of the tin with nowhere to go. His double rattlesnake technique was impressive to watch. And just as frost started to coat the outside of the shakers in his hands, the waiter stopped and poured. Eve first and then my glass. He wished us well with our first course, silently collected his things and disappeared. Eve smiled magnificently at me once we were alone with our obsidian jewels of fish eggs resting on a crystal platter accompanied by toast points and buckwheat blinis, whipped egg whites, crème fraîche and shallots. We each had our own mother-of-pearl spoon to serve ourselves.

"Did you find what you were looking for today?" Eve asked me, after lustily enjoying the first morsel of caviar.

I dug my spoon into the feast before us and spread the accoutrements onto a blini, adding the black pearls lastly on top. I stuffed the entire bite into my mouth and savored it.

"Actually yes," I said after I had swallowed. "Kind of anyway."

She leaned in with a smile, resting her chin on her palm. With her free hand she went in for more caviar. "That's so good!"

"Yeah," I agreed. "I didn't find the man I was looking for but I did find out where he is staying. So it should only be a matter of time."

Placing her hand on top of mine, a twinkle in her eye, she assured me that I would get him. Her smile was contagious and I could only smile back. Not wanting to bore her by talking shop, I changed the subject and we chit chatted through the rest of the first course. When every last orb was gone, the waiter came by once again and diligently removed the crystalline platter and our soiled utensils.

For her main course, Eve ordered a bone-in veal chop. I opted for the filet medallions with béarnaise. While waiting for our meal to be prepared, we had a bottle of champagne. Eve had ordered it, knowing what it was, wine still lost on me. A vintage Taittinger Blanc de Blanc. The bottle opened behind the scenes and emptied into the same type of carafe as the water being served on the floor, we were served the bubbles in the same kind of black Collins glasses as the water. Not as fancy as a flute or a coupe, but it got the job done. Our water was removed however, so as to not draw undue attention with an excess of glassware, and the champagne had to serve to quench our thirst.

We talked animatedly over the champagne as the bubbles started to go to my head. I was looking forward to the red wine we had chosen to accompany our entrees, as that was more my speed and it would ground me. The timing perfect, we took the last sips of the champagne just as our meals were severed; Eve's veal and potato soufflé and my steak with sauce béarnaise and artichoke hearts. The red wine was deep and voluptuous and went well with my filet. Eve was happy with her dinner choice as well.

My mind wandered back to earlier today when I thought about what kind of man Nice Guy Eddie might be. Sitting here, at *Steve & Mildred's,* one of the most expensive restaurants in the city, with the most stunning woman in the room, I couldn't help applying that same question about myself. Where I had come from, the choices I had made as an adult that kept me in that same rut. And then Prohibition struck and I was forced to change. And that change had led me on path that brought me here, to this moment, and this lifestyle.

I was getting accustomed and very seriously enjoying this high life. The other night when the Boss was describing precisely what Domaine Romanée-Conti was, I couldn't help but feel a twinge of jealousy because I wanted to try it, I wanted to taste it. The booze tasted better in this upper class. The steak tasted better. The women tasted better. And maybe it was the wine taking over but I couldn't wait to get out of here so I could fuck Eve again.

But before that would happen, Eve wanted a bowl of wild strawberries with lots of cream. The lady would get what she wanted.

In the Weeds

How the hell did I get here?

Bullets were whizzing by my head as cheap whiskey showered down on me. A bottle of said cheap hooch was in one hand, the .45 in the other. Out of frustration, mixed with a little *fuck you*, I threw the bottle in the direction of the people trying to kill me. Pulling the fedora down further, trying to keep the rainfall of whiskey out of my eyes, I needed to regroup and plan.

The heat and sulphuric smell of the blaze from the service truck I had just exploded by firing into the gas tank were slamming me like a wall, even with the protective barrier of the crates I was hiding behind. I had thought that blowing up the truck would prove me victorious, but I was still being shot at. Tommy guns are relentless that way. Luckily for me, the wind was not blowing the black and suffocating smoke in my direction, but rather towards the assassins. I had that going for me at least.

What a difference a day makes. Yesterday I had dined in one of Oldtowne's most luxurious restaurants and then went home and made love to the gorgeous woman who had accompanied me. Now people were trying to kill me. And doing a damn good job of it so far. After our tryst last night, I was glad that Eve needed to go home and left. Right now, I would give anything to be back in bed with her rather than in my current situation. She had needed to leave though, so I escorted her down the elevator of my building, through the lobby and out onto the sidewalk. I asked Warner, the doorman of my building, to hail Eve a cab. She was staring at the street, the dark asphalt damp and gleaming in the night.

"Eve," I said when I had finished with the doorman.

She didn't seem to hear me, lost in her own thoughts. I said her name again. She turned and flung herself at me. Her mouth hard and hot on mine. Lost in her, I didn't see or hear the taxi pull up to the curb. She must have known though, for just as quickly as she threw herself at me she pulled herself away from me, turned and jumped into the cab. I watched until the red taillights disappeared into the darkness. *What a woman!* She had left me feeling breathless.

"You're a lucky man, Mr. Hobbes," Warner complimented. I smiled in agreement and went back upstairs alone.

Her scent still lingered in my bedsheets when I awoke this morning. There was no time to be hot and bothered, though, as I received a wake up call from the front desk of my building saying that I had a message. The valet from the Dual Peaks hotel must have come through with something for me. I dressed hastily, wanting to get downstairs and hear the message. I skipped the shower and I skipped the coffee, two things I hate missing in the morning. It had rained overnight and the day was dreary. I threw on a trench coat over my clothes. And the fedora was just as much a shield in case it started to rain again as to hide my bed head.

Indeed, the Dual Peaks valet had come through. His name was Richard, my concierge Wade informed me. He had telephoned late during the night and said that he was sending a courier over with a message for me. The concierge then handed me a sealed envelope addressed to me that appeared untampered with. I tore it open as I made my way outside to fetch a taxi.

Reading the script that Richard had handwritten, my spirits had livened. I knew what Nice Guy Eddie was up to. And though there was no assurance in the letter that Eddie himself would be there, I would at the very least be able to throw a wrench in his scheme.

I tipped the cabbie double to speed over to the Boothby building so I could consult with the Boss. Pressing the gas, lurching me back into the rear seat upholstery, he did as I had bid. Skirting around early morning traffic and delivering me promptly, I made good with the extra cash.

My audience with the Boss, once upstairs, went as I had assumed it would. While I wondered what he was doing on the other side of that wall (Was he enjoying breakfast? Was he having a cup of coffee? And could I have a cup too?), I found it interesting that he was not surprised to see me at this hour. Nothing, it seemed, could puncture this man's cognizance. What *did not* surprise me, however, was that we had both reached the same conclusion about the valet's message and we were on the same page.

Nice Guy Eddie was going to attempt to sneak a truck full of hooch from Atlantic City to Kansas City through Oldtowne without paying the tariff to the Boss. And he was doing it tonight. Eddie's twenty four hours were up and the time for us to strike had presented itself. Richard had done his due diligence and had given us the When, the Where and the Time. And I would be there waiting to hijack it, Eddie's bootleg truck. Quick and easy. To be a fly in Nice Guy Eddie's ointment. To hurt his business. And to show him that he could not move through *our* town with impunity.

The plan was simple. I would lie in waiting ahead of time and stop the truck when it was passing by. I would then unload the contents of liquor and send the vehicle on its way; in a different direction to throw off the timeframe for the receiving end destination. Harry the Cat would then come by with a truck of our own and scoop the hooch and I up.

So that's how the hell I got here.

After leaving the Boothby building I returned home for a long, hot shower. A light rain had started so I donned the trench and the fedora once more and took myself out for a nice steak lunch. I didn't drink, only water and coffee, because I wanted to stay sharp. I met the Cat back at the Boothby building and he drove me out to the rendezvous point and then took off about a mile away to wait. Eddie's truck was due in about forty-five minutes, so Harry was to stay put for two hours. That would be plenty of time for the truck to come by and an hour for me to unload it, with fifteen minutes or so of leeway time.

During my tenure as a cop, I knew the ins and outs and Oldtowne intimately. But within the city proper; midtown, downtown, East Village ant the upper west side. Way out here, west on the outskirts of the suburbs, on the service road route Eddie had chosen to slink his contraband past, I was in unfamiliar territory. This stretch of highway was unknown to me and this neighborhood foreign. But I knew my way around my gun, and that was enough.

There were two shooters, I had by now discerned that much. And with the wind on my side, their bullets were coming less frequently and I could hear them hacking. That I wasn't contending with the Tommy gun for the moment was a relief. I chanced a look over the crates towards the position of the assassins and I could make one of them out. I fired in the direction of his coughing and took him down. That meant two were now dead, the driver of the milk truck being one of my contending villains of the moment in addition to the shooters, and just one left to deal with. When I had initially stopped the truck, standing in the middle of the street with my handgun pointed at driver's side of the cab which had forced him to pull over, I had tied up the driver and left him in the front seat. My intent had been to bind him while I unloaded the contents of the vehicle and then untie him and send him off once I had finished. That was before the two marksmen appeared, however. Now one of them was dead, as well as the driver who had certainly died in the explosion.

I could hear the cries of outrage from the second shooter, amidst his hacking, but I still couldn't see him. Taking another bottle of the whiskey, I flung it up into the air by where the sounds of him were coming from. Mid flight, I fired the .45 at the bottle, shattering it, raining fire and shards of glass down on my enemy. *This* drew him out. Surrounded by dark highway, a flaming inferno of a delivery truck, black smoke, and my gun, he had nowhere to go. He was the one who had the Tommy gun and when I saw him, I killed him.

And like that, with a sigh of relief, it was over.

I fell back on my ass in a pool of whiskey, but I didn't care. I was exhausted. The fire fight had taken a lot of energy out of me. Adrenaline had pumped through my veins, but now that it was over, I felt drained. The stillness did however give me time to think.

Where had those two gunmen come from? This was clearly an ambush and I had been set up. They knew exactly where I would be. How would they have even known about us hitting the truck? Only the Boss, Harry the Cat and I knew our plan…

And Richard the valet had given us the information. He had betrayed me.

He would have to wait for the moment though. Because where *had* those two gunmen come from? There must be a getaway car concealed around here somewhere, which meant that there was a possibility of a getaway *driver* still close out there who posed a threat.

And as I concluded this thought, I heard an engine screaming close. My sweat drenched hand clutched the hilt of my .45 tightly, waiting to deal with whomever was coming. The vehicle was bounding closer and the weariness I had felt moments ago disappeared as fear and adrenaline once again seared through my bloodstream. Raising my firing arm as it started to come into view, my index finger lightly coddled the trigger.

And then I relaxed and put my gun away. It was Harry the Cat, half an hour early. He slammed the truck to a halt, before reaching the delivery truck which was still ablaze. In seemingly the same moment, he leaped from the truck and shouted out for me. I raised myself from behind the crates and told him I was ok.

"What in the fuck happened?" He exclaimed.

I breathed heavily and told him I'd fill him in on the drive back. Accepting this, he continued to look around; taking in the explosion, the smoke, the two dead bodies.

"I didn't hear the explosion, but as soon as I saw all this smoke billowing up, I rushed right the fuck over here," he informed me.

I nodded. "Thanks, Harry."

"Thank God you're ok! I'm sorry I wasn't here sooner," the Cat was genuinely aggrieved by the situation and not being there to back me up.

"It's ok buddy, really it is," I assured him, "We couldn't have predicted this. And our plan was solid." He accepted this but was still bothered. "We may not be out of the woods yet though. There might still be a getaway driver around to deal with though."

Harry produced his own gun, his senses coming alert. "What should we do with all these crates?" He asked, motioning to the whiskey I had unloaded that we had been tasked to take back with us.

"Fuck it," I scoffed. "Leave it and let the cops deal with it."

With that, Harry and I got into his truck and drove back into Oldtowne without incident.

Drowned Sorrows

As I stepped back into the lounge proper of the *Ace of Clubs*, having just left the Boss' office, my shoulders sagged with the weight of the world. The drive back to the Boothby building from the scene of the crime was without incident. We never saw another vehicle out there so the getaway car must have fled. Had it been the black sedan of Eddie's driver? Probably. Our ride was silent; I didn't want to talk and Harry was respectful enough to not ask questions, though I know he wanted to hear the story. I would fill him in later. What I needed was quiet after nearly being killed. I had survived yes, killed the two men who were trying to kill me, blew up their service vehicle with half of their liquor stash and secured the other half. By all rights, I had won. Except I didn't. In the heat of the moment, I didn't realize that because I had been set up, that this was the second time Eddie had pulled one over on me. He was winning 2 to 0.

The Boss agreed that I should pay a visit to Richard the valet at the Dual Peaks as my next move. And while he had been mistaken before for thinking Nice Guy Eddie was of small consequence, the Boss now wanted this matter settled. For good. He considered the ambush as an act of war against his territory and our city. He was going to personally have a conversation with Enoch Johnson in Atlantic City, bypassing sending me up there for a conference. He was also going to dispatch Happy to stakeout the Dual Peaks for the first sign of our enemy.

The indistinct din of chatter and bells and whistles came from the casino floor behind me. I ignored the revelry in the room and was making my way towards the exit. I had to find Richard and ring his neck. It was my sole focus. That was why I never saw or heard Betty until she intercepted me.

"Jon, I've been calling your name," she told me, giving me a once over. She stood right in front of me and put her hands on my arms. "Are you ok?" There was genuine concern in her tone. I couldn't seem to find my voice.

"Jon." I still didn't respond, she was nearly as indistinct as the casino.

"Jon," her voice firmer. "You need to sit down."

That I comprehended. "No, I need to find the valet."

Her hands still on my arms, she gave them a light squeeze. "What you need, hunny, is a drink."

"No, I've got to find him."

Betty's liquid brown eyes bore directly into mine. "You'll get him, baby. But later. Right now you need to sit down."

"No," I said, with less assurance.

"Jon, let's go to the bar." She led me in the direction of my work station, where some kid who usually worked the bar upstairs and who's name escaped me at the moment, was tending my bar as he sometimes did in my stead when I was off duty or off on an adventure. I did as Betty ordered and she didn't need to guide me any longer. When we got there, I made to go behind my bar and prepare myself a drink.

"No, hunny," Betty stopped me and sat me down on a stool, belly up to the bar. "Let me do it for you." Again, I did as she bade.

Sitting, all that weight came crashing down on me. I could feel the clamminess of my skin from dried sweat and adrenaline. My hands and my face were filthy from soot and gunpowder. And my disheveled clothes hung like rags on my body. I needed a shower to freshen up. And as Betty placed a tumbler of a caramel brown liquid in front of me, she summed it up perfectly, "Jon you look like shit." Taking that first sip brought some sense back to me and I agreed. I stared at my distorted, rippled reflection at the bottom of the glass.

In my present state, I knew that my body would only be able to handle this one drink. Any more would go to my head; I was in too vulnerable a condition. World weariness pressed down upon me and as much as I needed to find the man who betrayed me and get some answers, now wasn't the time. The valet would have to wait. I needed to anchor and take care of myself before I'd be much good doing anything. Betty was right, and I was grateful.

Betty put me in a cab after my drink, which had done me some good. I was half drunk and half incoherent and all exhausted. After dozing in the cab, I got to my building and went up to my apartment. The shower cleansed me, washing away the weariness. But the exhaustion remained and my bed took me as I fell naked into it face first. There I remained, in a dark and dreamless sleep.

What a difference a day makes. The firefight had taken so much out of me. While last night I was determined to seek out the man who betrayed me, this morning I more clear-headedly saw the folly in that decision and am glad that I didn't follow through. Today, I was in a much better place both mentally and physically. My priorities were more in order.

First things first: coffee. I was still groggy, despite my deep sleep, but I was infinitely better than I was last night. A hot breakfast at the *Two Bits* was calling my name. Jet black coffee, eggs over easy and bacon burnt to a crisp. Toast slathered in butter and onion sautéed home fries, hold the ketchup. I needed to set myself aright before I began this quest. I had a long day ahead of me.

Showered and in fresh clothes, I made my way out of my apartment. Downstairs, making my way out to the street I exchanged pleasantries with my doorman, Warner, and he hailed me a taxi.

"Where to sir?" He asked, opening the taxi door for me so that he could give the driver a direction.

"The *Two Bits*," I told them both. A short ride but I'd be generous with the fare. Given that I never actually got any coffee yesterday morning to start the day off right, having it at lunch was too late, the damage had been done, and it fucked up my whole day (because we all know how *that* turned out), I didn't intend on making the same mistake twice.

Per usual, the *Two Bits* delivered in spades. The food was magnificent and What's Her Name kept my mug full. My breakfast was contemplative as I mapped out my day. The Dual Peaks with a word or two with Richard was preeminent on the To Do list. I was supposed to be on the bar tonight, but given that the Boss had escalated this situation into a declaration of war, he may call me off. I'd have to check in with him later this afternoon for instructions. And maybe by then he would have spoken with Enoch Johnson.

Now that I had my wits about me again, it was time to get things done. Properly. Outside the *Two Bits* was a telephone box. I picked up the receiver and the operator who sounded a bit like Marie Dressler patched me through to the number I requested. After a few rings, Harry the Cat picked up.

"Y'ello, the Cat speaking," he came through.

"Harry it's Hobbes." I didn't want to call Happy, as he was already busy scoping out the Dual Peaks and I didn't want to interfere. And besides, I owed Harry a story about last night. I told him where I was and asked him to come pick me up. I'd have him take me over to Eddie's hotel and he could be my backup or he could relieve Happy to get some rest, however it might play out.

"On my way, Hobbes," he assured me.

I went back inside the diner and ordered him an egg sandwich for the road. I was putting him out and I knew he'd appreciate it. It was also something to do to pass the time waiting for him. I had more coffee, this time with whiskey though. I wanted my nerves steeled.

Always seeming to have an appetite, the large man Harry the Cat accepted his sandwich gratefully and with awe that I would go out of my way to be so considerate. Like a maniac, he drove through the streets of Oldtowne, taking the freeway to the Dual Peaks. He drove with the sandwich in one hand and the steering wheel in the other. How he shifted gears was a mystery to me, and holding tightly onto the door handle for safety, I didn't want to know. Weaving in and out of traffic, unafraid of any cop who might pull us over, we would reach our destination in no time. Along the way I relived last night's events and filled him in on the details of the parts he had missed. He listened to the tale in silence, save for his chewing, and in the end was still apologetic about not having been there sooner to back me up. I assured him there was nothing to forgive and was grateful that he was with me on this today. With that, we were square. Except probably I was now one sandwich ahead and he felt he owed me one.

Harry didn't pull into the portico when we arrived at the Dual Peaks. Now that we knew Nice Guy Eddie was onto us, we didn't feel it safe to be front and center, exposed in plain sight.

Parking about half a block away, I got out of the coupe and made my way on foot to the valet station. The Cat was going to check in on Happy and see how he was holding up and if he knew anything yet. We were to meet back up in a few minutes.

Cautiously I made my way towards the front of the hotel, my mind on my gun. I could feel it's weight in the holster inside my coat. I wanted to be completely aware of it in case I were to suddenly need it. Being taken unaware again was *not* high on my priority list.

There were three valets on duty, that I could see. One was just driving off to go park a guest's vehicle, while another was returning from having completed the same task. And one guy was manning their workstation podium. Senses alert and my eyes scanning my surroundings for any sign of danger, I approached the valet station. Neither the man at the kiosk nor the man returning were Richard. My trained policeman's eye had spied the driver who was pulling away and I was 99% certain that he hadn't been Richard either.

The nameplate attached to the jacketed breast of the man at the dais read: Willie. Casually, I slipped my hand inside my jacket, as if I were reaching for a wallet or a set of reading glasses. The move was subtle and not meant to raise any alarm. But I was letting my fingers brush my Colt 1908. I was taking no chances.

"What can I do for you sir?" Willie asked. He probably assumed my hand was in my pocket searching for the voucher ticket for my vehicle to be fetched as I arrived at his station with no car.

Not to draw suspicion, I removed my hand and let it drop to my side. The side with the .45.

"I'm looking for Richard," I told him, keeping my voice neutral.

Willie grimaced and his face turned sour. "Richard didn't bother to show up for work today." The resentment in his voice was clear. "There's supposed to be four of us a shift to make everything run like clockwork, so now we're hustling."

Willie looked at my face intently for a moment, as if seeing me for the first time, and then recognition dawned there.

"You're Hobbes!" It was not a question. "You paid Rich a bunch of scratch for information!" I nodded but said nothing. "You think that's why he didn't show up today? He's got plenty of cash to quit this job?"

I had paid well for my information but not *that* well. And since Richard was clearly not here, I saw no reason to further entertain this conversation.

"Yeah, maybe," I indulged him and started to walk away.

"Is there anything I can do for you?" He called excitedly after me. I didn't need to see his eyes to know that they clearly went dollar green with greed. When I showed no sign of stopping, he clamored at my back, "Want me to tell Richard you were looking for him if I see him?" I gave no response to either question.

By this time, Harry had already touched base with Happy and was now running up a knoll towards me. Out of breath, he charged, "Hobbes, let's go," when he reached me. "We've got the driver."

Harry had parked his car illegally on the street at the bottom of the manicured lawn that led up to the front of the hotel. Grabbing my arm, the Cat pulled me and we raced together back down to his vehicle. Once inside, Harry roared his charge to a start and screeched off. He had been with Happy, who had been watching the car that Nice Guy Eddie and his man had taken here from Atlantic City. The same sedan that was at the dock and drove away with a case of the Boss' DRC. And most likely the same car that had fled from the wreckage on the outskirts of town during my firefight with two men and a milk truck. Nice Guy himself wasn't in it, but the driver was. As soon as he had gotten into his vehicle, Harry had come looking for me; which meant that he wasn't too far ahead. Happy was going to stay put just in case Nice Guy Eddie himself showed up.

Driving in typical Harry the Cat fashion, our vehicle dashed away to bridge the gap between us and Eddie's driver. It didn't take long to catch up to him, at which time Harry slowed and dropped back so we could follow him discreetly. He took to the freeway in pursuit, the taillights of the getaway car never out of my sight. Three cars back and driving casually, we trailed him. I was glad the Cat was with me on this, he was an amazing professional.

If the driver thought he was being trailed, he made no sign of it. His speed remained neutral and he made no evasive tactics. As he wasn't attempting to shake us, the best we could hope for was that he wasn't aware that we were following him. If he was aware of us, the worst case scenario, he was leading us into a trap. Either way, we were as ready as we could be.

Freeway pursuit was easy, as there were several cars traveling along as well. But as the driver made his exit on an off ramp, we'd have to be more cautious. The Cat was in control though; this wasn't his first day. A devious smile creased across his lips as he purposely drove by the exit.

Before I could voice my question, he assured me that he knew precisely where the driver was going. It took me a second, but then realizing where we were and what route the driver had taken, I knew exactly where he was heading too. And given that it was such a public place, the chances diminished that we were being led into an ambush.

Harry took the next off ramp up the highway. We would have to double back on some side roads, but this would lead us to our destination as well. *Saddlebred Club horse track.*

The amphitheater leading into the park was a gorgeous elongated structure with pristine whitewash and several steepled points of roof. An aesthetically pleasing building, the church-like venue was designed to attract the eye and offer hope, welcome you in… and take your money. Sure, winners walked out of the track everyday, but in the end, the House *always* wins. *God I fucking love this place.* The majesty of the horses. The skill and dedication of the jockeys. The elegance of the sport. The handicap. The thrill of the longshot. Having the inside track on the performances of the animals the day of the race and the state of course. *Wink.* This was one business that I had wished the Boss had gotten involved in.

Horse gambling in Oldtowne was run by the Sicilians however, and had been since the beginning of time.

After the Cat had suited up, checking and securing his weapon, we made our way inside, having purchased all access Grandstand tickets so that we could get a good visual to wherever Eddie's driver may be. The pretty young lady offered to rent us some binoculars, but Harry ever the professional, not to mention avid horse gambler, brought his own pair.

Scanning the floor inside, the driver was nowhere to be seen. A man on a megaphone trumpeted a two minute warning before a race was about to begin so the driver was probably outside somewhere on the bleachers getting ready for the dash to commence. My hope was that he'd be too preoccupied with his gambling affairs and so intent on his horse that he wouldn't notice us searching for him. Our window would be short though, as the race itself would only last a minute and a half.

I made a garb at Harry's elbow to get his attention and pointed up. He knew instantly what I meant. We made for the very top section, to seize the high ground and have the best vantage point. Quickly as we went, we had exhausted the two minute warning and we heard the gunshot for the race to commence before we made it out into the open air of the track.

From the dull concrete interior of the arena, it was a stark juxtaposition to the lush green grass of the field. The jockeys were low on their steeds as the horses rocketed, muscles rippling along the immaculately groomed turf of the track. It was a busier day here at *Saddlebred* than I had anticipated. We only had heartbeats before the race was over and the crowd would mass back in to collect their winnings; at which point we would lose the driver.

The Cat's eyes were already glued to his binoculars and I scanned the crowd as well. The thunder of the hooves crashing into the dirt and play-by-play by the man with the megaphone was a haunting minuet of our race against time. The horses roared around the bend getting ever closer to the finish line, their cannonade growing louder and causing the stands to tremble. The crowd began to roar, tickets waving in the air as if livelihoods were on the line. It would almost be exciting, if I had made a wager and didn't need to urgently find this *fucking* guy!

Harry's body went rigid. And I think we both must have spotted the driver at the same exact time. I nodded, assuring him that I saw him too. He was about three sections down but only one over. I pointed down at him, signaling that he should follow him from the outside while I ran back into the building to head him off. The winning horse crossed the finish line and was being announced over the amplifier. The Cat had already darted down the steps after him as I hauled ass to make it through the venue and down to the floor the driver would emerge on. I didn't want to lose him now.

Taking stairs several at a time, I sped downward. Before I exited the stairwell, I wanted to slow my pace and not draw any attention to myself. The driver could certainly identify me if he saw me and I didn't want to spook him. It was imperative that I catch him unawares. Coming out of the stairwell, I tread slowly and paused against the wall to get a good view. Eyeing the room and giving it a once and then second over, I actually got lucky with the full attendance of the track. The driver was in a long line at the betting counter to collect his score.

I moved in, discreetly standing only a handful of people behind him. Hopefully he would be concentrating on getting his money and would not notice me. But the gun at my side was ready to be drawn at a moments notice. As the line shuffled along, an announcement came over the PA that the next race would begin in thirty minutes. The driver glanced around, but it was that his intrigue was piqued, listening, and was most likely contemplating making a wager on another race and he still did not see me. I lowered my head anyway to look at the floor and turned away from him slightly. That was when I saw the Cat pretending to read the race boards nearby. He made a slight nod at me. As soon as the driver had his payout, I would intercept him and lead him into the Cat's direction.

At the window, the driver got his cash and then traded some back for the next score. Once his transaction was complete, he stepped aside to put his tickets in order. While sifting through his slips, I sidled along beside him and jammed the nose of my gun into his rib cage. His sudden abduction startled him, but not nearly as badly as when he saw that it was me who had done it.

"Let's go," I ordered.

We moved in unison. For the first few paces he was at peace and willing. But then I sensed his body start to tense, wanting to spring into action. And just as courage began to slowly course in his veins, the Cat stepped in tune behind us and the driver's will deflated.

"Where's Nice Guy Eddie?"

The Cat and I escorted the driver out to the corral, across the track, where the paddocks were, behind the barn. Near as I could tell, we were across the field from where we had been in the bleachers out in the northeast quadrant. The starting line was somewhere close between us and the arena.

Nice Guy Eddie. The driver. And Richard the valet.

The driver was the first of the trifecta we caught. It was my sincere intention to move quickly up that food chain. The driver on his knees in the dirt, Harry's pistol directed at him, I repeated my question.

"Where is Nice Guy Eddie?"

Out in the distance, words from a megaphone carried imperceptibly on the wind. The next race must be close to starting.

I had to give Eddie's driver credit. For a man who was about to die he was taking it well. Courageously. No blubbering, no bribe attempts. Nevertheless, he wouldn't answer my question. The Cat still had his cannon trained on him and I whipped my "Vest Pocket" out and pressed it to his kneecap.

"Please don't make me ask a third time," I implored.

"I don't know," he faltered. There was honesty in his voice, my years of listening to lying criminals confirmed this.

"Is he at the hotel? The Dual Peaks?" I pressed the barrel harder into his leg.

"No," the driver reported. "He has a room there but hardly stays there. I think he's got some dame somewhere and he shacks up with her. He only comes by when he needs me and gives me orders." He looked up at me pleadingly, knowing the excruciating pain of being shot in the knee and not wanting that for himself here and now. "Please," he implored right back. "I'm only on a need to know basis. Eddie gives me orders only when he's ready. I'm not even sure what the hell we're even doing here."

I considered this. "You weren't in the meeting when Enoch Johnson sent you guys down here?" I didn't honestly think this stooge would actually be at the sit-down, but it was worth a shot asking.

"Enoch Johnson?" He looked at me as if I were crazy. "Enoch Johnson has nothing to do with this. Eddie is breaking off on his own or something. He asked me to take him down here and said that it might get a little hairy. But I'd be paid well. But we had to do it without Johnson knowing. He'd kill us if he knew what we were doing."

"So, for the money, you decided to follow your Capo and at the risk of your life, quit Enoch Johnson's organization." It wasn't a question.

The driver nodded that this was correct.

My eyes hardened as the grip on my gun became tighter. "There's something you're not telling me," I assured him, also not a question.

A loud creak of the barn doors opening behind us signaled the march of the horses being led from the paddock to the starting gate. More white noise from the man on the megaphone and the distant rush of the crowd cheering; the horses were lining up.

"That's all I know. I swear!" Voice cracking, the driver pleaded.

The Cat's barrel went to the driver's temple. "I don't believe you," Harry threatened. A gun still making tactile contact with the driver's body, I was able to stand straight, remove my gun from his knee, and look down on him. I did not, however, put my gun away; just let it fall to my side.

"What are your next instructions? Is Eddie coming here?"

The driver tried to shy away from the cold steel pressed against his head. The Cat forbid it. Realizing whatever he did was futile, he answered, "No. I'm just here to blow off some steam. Day off if you will." I waited for him to go on. "I'm supposed to meet him at the hotel tomorrow night for the next assignment."

Time was a luxury we were now running short of, doing this interrogation in such a very public place. The diver was keeping things from me, that was for certain, but there was a lot of truth in his words as well. Reading between the lines and deductively piecing things together was pretty easy at this point. I believed that he didn't know any endgame or even the full scope of why he was here. He was blindly following Eddie's orders from operation to operation. But I was getting the feeling that Eddie wasn't at the top of this totem pole and that his instructions were coming from somewhere as well. And *not* Enoch Johnson.

Then who?

I was convinced that this was all I'd be getting out of him about Eddie. And besides, I now knew where he would be tomorrow night. I'd be there waiting and ready for him. Time to change direction. "Where's the valet? Richard." I would need to pay closer attention to his tells here, for as the driver and lackey he was most likely the one who had direct contact with Richard.

Grimacing, the driver closed his eyes. I don't think he anticipated being asked about the valet. His silence vexed me. "Is he *here?" Waiting to ambush us...* I didn't complete the thought aloud. The hairs on the back of my neck tingled and the Cat started to look around, gun never leaving the driver's head. This would be a dangerous situation now if the driver's accomplice was also here as well, in hiding.

"No," he said with finality. My gaze bore into him suspiciously, cautiously. Surmising the truth here was important; to ensure we weren't in any immediate danger.

"The valet is dead." Harry continued to search around, but still there was no one to be seen. "We used him as a tool, giving him false information we knew would get back to you."

So if this was true, Richard the valet was not our enemy and had not betrayed me. If untrue, this would be the moment he would strike.

The driver concluded his story, "Once you took the bait about the delivery truck, we fed him to the fishes."

No ambush came. The three of us were still alone out here, save the horses and jockeys about fifty yards away and the crew securing them at the starting gate. I closed my eyes and sighed. Richard had done what I asked him to do and he had paid for it with his life. We had *all* been set up by Eddie. Eddie, the only player left now. Unless of course my instincts were correct and that he had someone to report to as well. Either way, I was now on the final stretch.

My ears pricked to listen to the far off man on the megaphone. It was over and all three of us knew it. The countdown was on and declining from ten. The driver clenched his eyes and prepared for the arrival of death.

5,

4,

3,

2,

Coinciding with the cap shot in the air from the starting pistol, signaling the fast break of the steeds out of the gate and onto the track, Harry the Cat fired his own gun into the driver, drowning out the loud bang of death.

And they're off.

If You Have to Ask How Much it is, You Can't Afford It

Now that I knew where Eddie would be, and when, I decided to get some rest and leave everything be until tomorrow. This way I would be refreshed and alert for my confrontation with my nemesis. The Cat and I resisted our urge to stay at the track and bet on some horses, but committing murder, especially on the property, would do that.

With the barn empty, everyone busy with the current race and the following accolades and prizes and flower giving, we dragged the driver into the barn and stuffed the body under the hay of a stall. There was no need to be too detailed or overly careful with hiding the body; there was nothing to tie some low-level hood from Atlantic City and his corpse being dumped at a horse track in Oldtowne to us. We would be long gone, with no evidence connecting the deceased to us, by the time he was found. And once he was discovered, suspicion would focus on Atlantic City, not Oldtowne.

We stopped back at the Boothby building and in the *Ace of Clubs* to report to the Boss, where we had a mandatory drink before going in to see him and then another on our way out. What can I say, I'm not a man who can resist when a woman hands me a glass of hooch, especially *my* girls who run around my cocktail area in my own environment. They even know just what I like.

Betty was off tonight, I would have liked to have seen her. I was feeling sentimental for some reason, after the act of violence the Cat and I had committed. Vivian and Julia were acceptable substitutes in her absence, however, gorgeous women happily serving me the brown water of life. I even searched around the bar for a glimpse of Eve, but she wasn't to be found either. I sighed into my glass, hoping no one would notice.

But once our debrief and forced happy hour was over, it was time for me to go home and sleep. I would need my rest and preserve some energy for tomorrow. I intended to finish this. Harry was going to do the same, except first he was going to head to the Dual Peaks and pull Happy off of surveillance duty and take him for something to eat; he too had had a long day, just perhaps not as long as ours. I shook Harry's hand once our whiskey was through and thanked him for tagging along with me today. He nodded and nothing further needed to be said.

The taxi I had called was waiting for me by the curb, idling in the night as I exited the Boothby building. I gave the cab driver my address and directed him to take me home. Pulling away from the curb and into the light traffic of the late evening, we began to make our way. By the time we hit the top of the street, I had changed my mind.

"Take me to Cooper's Garage," I ordered and giving him the address to the new destination. He altered his route and we sped away.

Earl Cooper, proprietor of Cooper's Garage would be in when we got there, I knew. Earl lived, breathed and worked at his shop and very rarely left. He was also caretaker to one of my finer possessions. And for tomorrow I would want it. The shop wasn't too far out of our way and when we arrived I paid the fare and tipped generously. The cabbie asked me if I wanted him to wait so he could take me home after I conducted whatever after hours business I had here, not that he cared he said. But I politely declined.

"I'm a cop," I assured him, stretching the truth probably a bit too far. As for the ride home, I wouldn't be needing one. Tipping his hat and thanking me for the business, the cab driver took off to his next customer.

Cooper's Garage stood like some ramshackled outbuilding with weathered wooden planks and a large overhead bay door. Despite its clumsy appearance, Earl Cooper had this place reinforced and fortified. He also had a pair none too friendly German Shepherds and an American hammerless shotgun; this was not the place you wanted to be caught trespassing. At the top of the structure was a large sign that read *Cooper's* and beneath it was a friendly, ball capped caricature of a grease monkey that looked remarkably nothing at all like the man himself. And underneath the mechanic, completing the sign was *Motor Garage*.

Cooper and I went way back, he had known my father and was a lifelong family friend. He had taught me how to drive and showed me how to work on cars. And once Prohibition hit and I came into a business that paid *real* money and not the peanuts of a lawman's salary, he had introduced me to the contacts I needed to buy my baby. A Rolls Royce Phantom 1 Jonckheere Coupe, black as midnight with red leather interior. I housed my vehicle here at the garage, under Cooper's charge. He kept it locked away in a secure recess of his building, where he maintained it and kept it in pristine condition.

I traipsed up the graveled path that led to a door beside the rolling metal entryway. The instant my knock landed, the dogs began. Loudly. Ferociously. Next there was a snap and a floodlight blazed on, illuminating the entire front courtyard and me as an intrusion. Even above the clamor of the dogs I could hear the distinct cock of the shotgun, my hearing honed from years of my profession. Not until all this happened, did Earl address the intruder at his door.

"It's me, Coop," I identified myself, "Hobbes."

When he opened the door for me, the shotgun was no longer in his hands but the dogs still barked. There was however a chain still locking the slightly ajar door.

"Back again so soon?" He inquired through the crack in the door. This was the second time this week I had come for my car, which was unusually frequent for me. I had used it the other day while exploring the city in search of which hotel Eddie may have been hiding in.

I nodded. "I'm gonna need her for tomorrow," I told him, "Where I'm going, I'm gonna need to arrive in style. Besides, she's my good luck charm."

Cooper understood immediately, but was a man who knew not to ask questions. He raised a finger, asking me to wait a minute. He closed the door and shushed the dogs back then undid the chain. Reopening the door, he invited me inside.

"Cup o' joe?" He offered, as I followed him inside his warehouse.

"No. Thanks." I had a long day tomorrow and would be wanting my bed soon, without the interference of caffeine.

"Something a bit stronger then?" He turned and winked over his shoulder and I knew he wouldn't let me refuse this time.

In his desk there was a key to the lockbox on the wall beside him, that secured the keys to my Phantom. In a trick drawer beneath where he kept the key to the lockbox was a bottle of whiskey and two tumblers. He took out of the desk the necessary ingredients for our exchange and he poured some golden amber into the greasy looking glasses. Whatever medicinal properties and cures that whiskey promised, I was going to need all of them to survive drinking out of the glass offered me. We clinked and downed it. After our *cheers* (and a silent prayer that I wouldn't come down with the plague), Cooper retrieved the keys to my Phantom and dropped them reverently in my palm.

"She's gassed up and ready to go," he assured me. He always kept her pristine for me.

Closing the keys in my hand, I thanked him and thanked him again for the whiskey. Declining politely another shot, I made my way to the alcove that housed my car. It too was hidden behind a locked metal rollaway door. On my key ring were three keys and a bullet shell from the first man I killed after I was no longer a cop.

I had kept it as a souvenir, a trophy, and a tangible reminder that I can never go back. Chiseling out a tiny hole to slip the ring through, the empty bullet clinked against the three keys.

Key one was a mortise key that unlocked the gate behind which was my Phantom coupe. The second key had a large square bow with the letters *RR* raised on the gold plate surface and the word *Rolls* etched above the double letters and *Royce* below. Obviously, that one brought my girl to life. And the third key, well, well it… well it certainly wasn't the key to my heart.

Using the mortise passkey, I unlocked the clasp and rolled the gate up. There she was. In all her beauty. Flirting with me, teasing, just by sitting there. An enticing sheen on her raven body. Alluring curves, like a woman. Her interior lipstick red waiting to be kissed, *hard.* Gently, I brushed the back of my hand against her. How could you not admire such a bewitching thing?

Her name was *Audrey Manhattan,* so called after exposition girl and actress Audrey Munson, the first female to ever grace the silver screen of Hollywood fully in the nude. Like an American Venus, her full milky form and every ounce of her sensuality sashayed in movie houses across the land, burning the image of her nudity into the collective conscious of the country; whether for excitable good or lascivious evil. I had been entranced since I had seen the film *Inspiration* a decade ago when it was released. Munson had gone on to be called by most as 'Miss Manhattan'. I took that epitaph and added her first name to it and dubbed my vehicle as the *Audrey Manhattan,* since both the woman and my Rolls were the epitome of indulgence and gratification.

I slid into the driver's seat, inserted the gold key and brought her purring to life. She responded to me as if we were made for one another, and like the pretty lady she was, I brought her home.

All About Eve

The building I lived in was called the Channing building. I pulled the *Manhattan* onto my street, an avenue bedecked with high rise office buildings and luxury apartments that rose up like hotels; boxes of people stacked on top of each other, surrounded in creature comforts. Lights shone from windows intermittently from the length and height of the many buildings like tiny diamonds, pinpricks of luminescence escaping through the dark fabric of night. As I turned my girl silently to the curb before my building, Warner, my doorman, made his awestruck way to the edge of the sidewalk, as close to the car as he dared.

Leaving her running, I got out of the Rolls and saw Warner's marveled expression.

"You know, Mr. Hobbes," he began, "Seeing this car never gets any less magnificent, no matter how many times you bring her here."

I had to smile at his admiration. His eyes sparkled like some little kid on Christmas morning. "Park her for me, will ya?" I asked. This made his day. It always did.

As Warner hurried around the front of the vehicle to get in, ecstatic to get behind the wheel and bring her into the building's garage, I made my way inside, leaving him to his bliss. Brightly lit and opulent, the foyer was grand with its marble floor and simple artwork adorning the walls. Potted plants and decorative couches populated the room, finishing out the lobby. Such a far cry from my triple decker upbringing. I didn't see Wade, the concierge, he must be off for the evening, but Wallace was behind the front desk. I waved when he greeted me and continued on to the elevator.

Two golden doors with raised etchings of some Greco-Roman architecture provided the entryway onto the lift, as if they were leading you up to heaven itself. I pushed the *Up* button and watched as the dial on the numbered half circle of the indicator above the doors slowly brought its *fleur-de-lis* needle down to the 1. As ever, Wilson was there when the doors slid open, manning his post. His uniform was a deep velvet maroon, both slacks and top to match, with a double-lined golden stripe running up the pants leg and a matching set wrapped around the collar. On his head was the small, boxy bell cap, the same maroon and material. From clavicle to waist was a line of buttons on either side of the body, like suspenders. White gloves covered his hands.

"Watch your step getting in please," Wilson cautioned. As always.

He didn't ask me what floor I was going to, a professional at his job, he never needed to. As he pulled the lever that started the lift, he bid me a good evening and inquired about my day. We made the usual small talk, after I had told him my day had been good I asked him the same. His response was the same as mine. There was a stool in the corner for Wilson to rest from being on his feet all day, but it occurred to me that I had never seen him use it. I wonder if he ever did. It also got me to thinking about my upbringing; we had been a poor family growing up and I was blue collar, literally, as an adult. And now *this*.

I had driven a Rolls Royce, *my* Rolls Royce, to the upper west side, the ritzy part of Oldtowne where I lived. In a building that had staff, from the sidewalk outside all the way up to my door. It was unbelievable. Sometimes I would pinch myself as I enjoyed the view out of my window to the beauty of the Oldtowne city scape just to make sure it was real. Some of my old cop buddies, the ones who wouldn't bust me until they *had* to but didn't want to know any of the details of my new life either, thought it was blood money. But not me. No, I was living proof of the American Dream.

"Your lady friend is quite striking," Wilson intoned, bringing me back to the moment. He was referring to Eve, who had been here several times now.

With a *ding* we had reached my floor and stepping out I thanked the elevator operator for his service and his compliment.

"Be sure to watch your step when exiting, please."

I nodded a good night and turned my key into my apartment door and stepped inside. Something was wrong. I sensed it immediately. Someone had been in here. And maybe he still was. Adrenaline kicked in and my body tensed. The .45 was in my hand without even having to think about it. Quietly and slowly, cautiously, I made my way around the apartment after I had silently secured the door behind me so that I would not be ambushed from anyone who might be outside in the corridor. The kitchen was clear, save a soiled old fashioned glass that I hadn't used sitting on the counter, a sip of liquid still glistening at the bottom. Whoever had broken in had helped themselves to some of my booze. *Fucker*!

Moving into the living room, there was no one in there either. The curtains had been drawn open though, exposing the nighttime view I enjoyed so much; something else I hadn't done. Raising my weapon, I made for the bedroom, the closet and the bathroom as two blind spots that the intruder or intruders could use as hiding places and attack. I was calm and ready, but a bead of cold sweat ran down the back of my neck.

My pistol still elevated, ready to fire and defend myself at any moment without hesitation, I wondered who the trespasser could be. Had Nice Guy Eddie actually broken into my apartment and was right now waiting to kill me in my own bedroom? Had he found out about his driver already and was here to retaliate and take his revenge? Since his arrival in Oldtowne he had been at least one step ahead of me the entire way. That sweet taste of victory I had savored all day from a job finally well done, with the disposal of the driver and knowing Eddie's next whereabouts, turned sour in my throat now. It was always going to come down to Eddie and me, I had just hoped that it would have been tomorrow, on my terms.

And that was when the third thing that was out of order presented itself, just as I was about to cross the threshold into my room. I could smell it. I could smell *her*. Eve's perfume, her intoxicating scent. And there, sleeping in my bed, was the outline of a woman beneath my covers. Eve the Sensation's form. When Wilson had complimented me on scoring a dame like Eve, I had assumed that he had meant it in general, not that she was actually here, tonight, right now, in my apartment. In my bed.

Returning the gun to its holster at my side, I softly made my way to the bed so as to not startle her. None of the staff in my building had alerted or informed me that Eve was up here. Had she not been sleeping and instead stepped out in front me, I could have killed her in my startle. Then again, there was the elevator operator who made his compliment. And Wallace at the front desk may have tried to tell me, but I had passed him by with just a bid of goodnight. And of course there was Warner, who must have been so enamored with the Rolls that it slipped his mind to inform me that Eve was upstairs in my apartment.

Reaching her, I stroked her cheek gently and ran my fingers through her hair. I bent so that my lips were close to her ear and I whispered, "Goldilocks." She didn't stir. "Goldilocks," I said again gently. "Goldilocks wake up."

This time she did.

When I had come into the room and saw that it was Eve who had trespassed into my home, my body had relaxed and I was no longer on the defensive. But as she woke and turned over to face me, smoldering eyes run messy with mascara and tears, a black and blue raccoon circle covering her half closed left eye and a swollen red cheek upon her impossibly gorgeous countenance, my body went rigid once again at this greeting, my blood came to a boil and I was ready to kill whomever had struck this beautiful creature.

For a long moment we just stared at one another. I knew my face was teeming with rage, but the look on hers was something... else. Something I couldn't quite place. Consternation? Mistrust? I thought I knew a thing or two about women. She was wounded and vulnerable right now. She would want me to take her in my strong arms and kiss her; to assure her that she was safe now, that everything would be alright, that I was here to protect her. But as I reached in to envelop her, she put a delicate hand to my chest, stopping me.

"No," she mouthed through newly minted tears.

I didn't understand, I couldn't. Isn't this why she had come? Because I made her feel safe? As she slowly started to get out of my bed, I put my hand on her shoulder. I was going to attempt an embrace again, to shield her.

"*No.*" This time more definitive.

Flinching away from her as if I had been stung, my hands shot up in a surrendering defense mechanism. She wouldn't even turn to face me.

"I'm not going to hurt you, " I assured. I thought I heard her scoff, but I couldn't be sure. *What the fuck is going on here?* At a loss of what to do, I asked who had done this to her.

She was out of the bed now, but on the other side, the mattress between us. Finally she turned to look at me. Her face was bruised and the skimpy dress she wore was disheveled and tattered. The look I couldn't describe a moment ago had hardened and was solidified. There was hate there, but whether for me or the person who did this to her or both of us I couldn't be sure.

I stood from the bed for our face off. I didn't know what to say. I didn't know what she wanted, needed, me to do. This was a game that was out of my league. I didn't know who would win our standoff or even how to play. The distance between us now was miles and those sapphire eyes of hers that I loved were no longer sparkling nor could I penetrate them. We were strangers, I realized suddenly. I had been falling for her and I didn't even know it, until now. Now when she had cut herself off from me, taken herself away. I didn't love her, of course, not yet, but I knew that I could eventually get there. I had been entranced by her magnificent beauty, her mystery and allure. She could drink like I can and the chemistry we had in bed, now our battlefield, had been undeniable.

Eve knelt to retrieve something from the floor, something I couldn't see. Was she going for a gun? Would she try to kill me? Would I let her?

She came up with the strap of a high heel clutched in her hand and bent her leg to put it on. She then secured the second. None of this was making any sense to me. What could I do? Why had she even come here if she was going to act this way? I went for one last ditch attempt.

"Let me take you out of here," I implored. "We can go get something to eat or a drink and you can tell me what happened."

A crack appeared in her stoniness. Taking advantage of this fissure of emotion, I began to move toward her around the bed.

"Where would we go?" She asked, her voice cracking too. Her fingers went to her face. "No. No I can't be seen in public like this."

In the short steps it took me to reach her, I knew that I had won. I wasn't sure how, but I had. Now certainly I could take her in my arms. Everything else we could figure out later. But the moment I touched her, the cracks resealed and grew stronger.

"No!" She screeched fiercely and fled from the room.

She was quick, Eve, I'd give her that. She was through my apartment and out the front door in heartbeats. I pursued, wondering why now, but went after her anyway. She couldn't get far once out in the hallway. She would either have to wait for the elevator or take her chances down multiple flights of stairs. Either way, I would catch up.

But more of my bad luck struck when I made it out into the corridor. The elevator was already on my floor and open, Wilson warning to watch your step, as Eve darted inside.

Fuck.

Are you fucking kidding me!

After banging my fist on the sealed elevator doors, once I made it there, I made for the stairs and dashed down them. Taking them several at a time, I couldn't believe I was actually doing this. What was wrong with her? What was wrong with *me*? On the ground floor of the lobby, I barged through the exit door of the stairwell and raced across the marbled tile. Charging through the revolving door out on the street I searched frantically for Eve.

"Is everything alright, Mr. Hobbes." The doorman, Warner, inquired. "The lady looked pretty shaken up."

"Where did she go?" I demanded.

Warner was taken aback by my sternness. Flustered, he said, "She- she got in that cab." And pointed at the one driving off up the street.

"Get my fucking car!" I barked. And Warner scurried away to follow my orders, this time not as excited to get behind the wheel of my Rolls I was sure, as I watched the fading taillights of the vehicle taking Eve away from me.

Bullets on Broadway

If I had known I was going to be up all night, chasing Eve all around the goddamn city, I would have taken Cooper up on that cup of coffee. All my frustration slammed the gas pedal of the *Manhattan*, the full weight of my body pushing down one leg. The Phantom went from zero to 60 in 3.5 *fuck you*'s that I shouted in rage, as I floored the vehicle after nearly tossing Warner bodily from the round door of the car and in the direction Eve's cab had gone.

In pursuit, I had lost precious time as the doorman had gone to fetch *Audrey*. Luckily, the streets would not be as crowded at this hour. And besides, the Rolls Royce could go significantly faster than any Studebaker taxi. I was angry, no *furious*, but at whom? Eve? The man who had assaulted her? Myself? Regardless, I was taking it all out on the pavement.

In the moments I was waiting for my doorman to retrieve the *Manhattan*, I followed the direction the cab was taking, getting further from view. Moving north away from me, it took a left at the top of the lane. It wasn't much to go on, but it was a start. I tore up the avenue and pitched around the same left. There was a limited amount of places they could be heading going in that direction.

The park was out that way, but they would be exposed at this hour going there. The only other thing coming to mind was that they were leaving the city and heading out to the Palisades or... or they were going to double back, in which case they could go anywhere and I would most likely lose them.

I took my chances going north west, and I would make a loop around the park. Maybe I would get lucky. There were plenty of apartments and hotels out this way, and mansions the further north into the Palisades you went. Eve surely being wealthy, and the little I knew about her, could certainly afford to live somewhere in this section of town. If indeed home was where she was going.

Eve. Who had done this to her? And why? Who even was she? A mystery to be sure. Clearly she was a socialite of some kind, and monied, to have been allowed access into the *Ace of Clubs*. She had come into my bar and indulged on martinis and cognac and then I had indulged on her. But really what else did I even know about her? She wore no wedding ring, but that didn't necessarily mean she wasn't married. The shape of a ring may be eternal but it slips off a finger easily enough. Is that who had done this? Her husband? Had he found out about our affair and punished her? Or had it been some jealous boyfriend? A scorned lover who she had left for me and he beat her for it? I was so wrapped up in the sex of it all that I never thought of the real world and all its problems could penetrate our frivolity and wantonness. It had been a fantasy.

A fantasy that had been dashed when I saw Eve's broken face.

So consumed was I with lust that it never occurred to me to ask her questions. Questions that reached beyond small talk. Had I actually learned anything about her, beyond each curve of her naked body, then maybe I would now have an inkling as to where she might be headed. What good was the memorization of the shapeliness of her tits, the pale pink color of her nipples, doing me now?

That raised another question. She was a great lay sure, but was I *actually* falling for her? Or was I just falling for the damsel in distress routine? I was out here in the middle of the night, driving with no clear direction, to try to track down a person who may not even want to be found. But then why had she come to my place? Why had I found her in my bed?

Clutch, shift, and I pressed the accelerator harder.

I had only passed one vehicle, and it wasn't a cab, by the time I reached the south side of the park. Each passing moment without locating her broadened Eve's escape and likelihood that I would not find her. If she had had the taxi driver double back and head south down towards midtown, the earth would swallow her and I would have no chance of finding her until she wanted to be found again. *If* she wanted to be found again. Or was she fleeing the city? Heading north and leaving Oldtowne behind?

Turning right, I started circling the park. Most lights were already out with more being extinguished. Radio knobs were being switched off in homes, folks finished listening to programs like *The Clicquot Club Eskimos* or the *Waldorf-Astoria Orchestra*. Decent people were climbing into their beds or already fast asleep, while the sinners were fucking and the delinquents drinking.

Offenders were drunk in this part of town from tucked away caches of liquor that they had hidden from authorities and refused to give up; there were no speakeasies this far north in Oldtowne.

Making a complete round of the park, I saw a set of tail lights up ahead. I was already at a roaring speed so I would come upon and overtake the car rather quickly. As I grew closer I could make out the Studebaker form and could see the yellow and black checkers on the side panel indicating that it was a taxi.

Yes!

The car was making no attempt at evasive action or to try to allude me. Nor was it speeding up to make a getaway. Because of this, the momentary elation I had felt that this was the cab Eve was in started to fade. Unless of course they just didn't see me. Coming upon them, I pulled up along side. Sure enough, the cab had a fare, but it wasn't Eve. Thanks to Oldtowne for taking a queue from the New York Taxi Service and wanting to be a grown up city like New York, we had our own *fleet* of taxicabs. The likelihood that this had been Eve's car had been slim to none; even at this late hour. I had just been hopeful.

Bypassing the checkered car and my loop of the park complete, I was at a complete loss. There was nowhere to go, nowhere else to search. I was certain that Eve had had the cab double back. I may not know much about her, but I knew that she wasn't a stupid woman. What was my next move? Where should I go next?

To bed came to mind. I was out here on this fools errand, when really I had a big day tomorrow. I finally had Nice Guy Eddie in my grasp. Eve and her mysteriousness would have to wait. Sighing, I knew it was hopeless. I had no chance of finding her tonight and would have to wait until she came back to me, if she were to ever come back to me.

I decided to drive back home, but I'd take the long way around. I'd head in that direction but I'd continue my search until I got there. Going slowly and not taking the direct route, I zigged and zagged and maneuvered up and down different streets as I angled back towards the Channing building. The park of the northwest pocket of Oldtowne and the taxi that Eve had *not* been in long behind, I found no trace of her by the time I was halfway home. And I had not expected to.

At a relatively new invention, and certainly new to us in Oldtowne, something called the tricolored traffic light, I stopped at an intersection where the top bulb glowed red. Headlights blazed in my rear view mirror, causing me to squint and distracting me from contemplating what was going on with Eve and where she could have gone. I was at a complete stop and obeying the traffic laws. But the vehicle behind me was coming at me too quickly for my comfort.

I kept glancing uncomfortably into the rear view mirror as the car was getting closer. My instincts were kicking in and telling me to get the hell out of there. But I ignored them, wanting to play this out. What were the chances that this jerk was out here looking for me? Probably he was just some punk or drunkard going too fast at night.

At the last minute before colliding with my rear end, the car swerved and pulled up to the light beside me. It was a Packard Single Six with the added addition of a top light attached to the roof of the car, a light that shone as red as the stop light we were at now. Glancing over to my left for a better look, I didn't know the man in the passenger seat but I certainly knew the officer behind the wheel.

Sciarra. Great.

Officer Sciarra of the Oldtowne police department in his Packard squad car was parked next to me and he was eyeing me down. As if he had known he would find me here. And given the speed he had advanced upon me, I was pretty sure of it. *Curious.* Did Eddie have a contact in the department and had he sent them to shake me down? Or did this have something to do with Eve somehow? I have a hard time swallowing coincidences. And having Oldtowne PD show up *now* to harass me was just too much to take in. But then again, how would *anyone* know that I was out here in the *Audrey Manhattan* looking for Eve?

Sciarra and I never got along, even before Prohibition and we were on the force together. Not everything was roses and brotherly in the fraternal order of the police department. There were plenty of rivalries within the ranks of the force and I had had my fair share. Sciarra was probably my greatest enemy within the force. And a patrol car showing up here, now, *especially* Sciarra, made me very uncomfortable.

Both Sciarra and his young partner were eyeing me. The partner was trying his best to be discreet about it, but not Sciarra. Behind the wheel, Sciarra's mean mug was targeted right at me. *What the hell is going on here?* My mind was racing to figure out what this could all be about. Eve? The Nice Guy Eddie situation? The murder of Eddie's driver earlier this afternoon; there's no chance they could have linked that back to me. There was no evidence, I had made sure of it. What then? The *Ace of Clubs*? Were they finally cracking down on our illegal hooch parlor? Or had Sciarra happen to notice my car out for a late night joyride in the mostly deserted streets of Oldtowne and decided to break my balls?

The light went green and I shot off. There was no way that the Packard could keep up with my Phantom. Nothing about this situation was kosher, nothing about it I liked. Sciarra was up to something, I was sure. No way did he just chance upon me. However, I didn't like running from the police, it brought too much undue attention. In the past five years since my departure from the force, I made it a point to always be obedient and complicit with any run-ins I may have with the police, even the officers I hadn't been friendly with. That was my procedure and the Boss' orders. While the department may turn a blind eye to whatever it was they thought I was up to given my history with them, it would only get me so far. I still had to be cautious. But something was wrong here, something was definitely fishy. I just didn't trust Sciarra.

I had blasted off, leaving Sciarra trailing behind. Not that it mattered. Because a couple of blocks up I learned that my instincts had been correct. To my detriment. Another squad car had been hidden, lying in wait around a corner. Luckily for me I had seen him at the last minute so I could swerve around him as he pulled out and tried to block me in. The driver was Brandt, one of Sciarra's cronies. Sciarra was still in hot pursuit behind me and Brandt turned to pursue as well. As soon as the pair of them joined the chase, the cherry tops on the roof of their cars blazed on and the horn of sirens began to roar.

Whatever the hell was going on here, I would have to figure out later. Right now I had to escape these two. *Goddamn Eve.* If she hadn't come over tonight, if she hadn't run out, I wouldn't be in this mess right now. I'm supposed to be in bed getting rest for tomorrow!

Flooring it, I tore up the road. And that's when another patrol car flew out at me from an intersecting street. I didn't get a good look at who was behind the wheel, but if I had to guess, I'm sure it was Latrelle; another adversary of mine from back in the day. Latrelle, if indeed it was him, had caught me off guard and when I swerved so as to not collide with him, I lost momentary control of my car. A splash was made in my stomach when my heart fell into it and I caught my breath again only when I was able to regain control and right the car.

With three of them after me now, I made a hard right at the next corner, tires screeching in rage as I fishtailed. The Rolls Royce Phantom 1 Jonckheere Coupe was sleek and aerodynamic, but as fast as she could go, sharp turns, especially at lower speeds, were a struggle. Good thing I was going fast. I knew this maneuver wouldn't lose them, but it should slow them down. They would have to brake hard and then be bottlenecked, turning onto this new avenue one at a time. That should buy me some time.

With the few seconds I had purchased, and with a thin hope that there were no more cars ahead waiting in ambush, I needed to figure out my next move. Where would I go? Home was too obvious and therefore too dangerous. The *Ace of Clubs* was a nonstarter, there was no way I was going to lead them to the Boothby building. The *Two Bits* was open 24 hours, but I didn't think it safe to stay out exposed in a public place for too long.

I needed to disappear. And the best place to hide a needle was *not* in a haystack, but with other needles. What I needed to do was get to a more populated area of town. And while we weren't New York, the city that never sleeps, Oldtowne was still grown up enough to have a moderate amount of traffic buzzing, even at this late hour; especially in midtown and downtown. I wasn't fool enough to think that my Phantom would blend in with other commuters, nor that I would lose my pursuers this way, but it would make it more difficult for them to capture me. I turned south and headed towards midtown.

In a few minutes I saw the flash of a red light and then another. They were trailing me. I was too far ahead for them to catch up, I'd have to lose them turning this way and that up and down streets. My old troop in their squad cars had no chance of bridging the gap between us… but their bullets did. They had fired, what I took to be a warning shot, just beside me, reminding me that indeed they *could* catch up to me if they so chose.

More shots. So help me god if they hit my car. But for now they were just firing warnings, trying to get me to stop, pull over. Hands clutched tight around the steering wheel, teeth gritted, and the pedal as far into the floor as she could go, I did my best to outrun the bullets. One struck home. It whizzed right be the driver's side window like a miniature tornado and struck the rounded top of the cover over the wheel. *Mother fuck!*

Inventing new curse words for these bastards who were chasing me, I had been distracted by the blasts coming at me. Their red siren lights were like beams from hell hunting me in the night. And that was when, looking in the rear view back at them, that Sciarra had pulled his Packard out of nowhere and was upon me. He must have separated from the group and used Brandt and Latrelle and their bullets as a distraction so he could maneuver freely and sneak up on me from a side street. Basically it was the same tactic that they had already used. And I fell for it. Again.

Racing into the intersection and coming straight at me, while bullets still whirred from behind, Sciarra tried to ram me. But I wouldn't let him. I swerved hard and flew past him, but he was right on my tail and the other two cruisers gained a notch during the heartbeats it took for me to slide by Sciarra. All three patrol cars were on me again, beacons of red flashing off of the black paint of my car and sirens deafening.

While they had succeeded in gaining traction and closing the distance between us, it only took me a moment to gather speed and break away again. My best defense here was that their Packards could never keep up with my Phantom. Tearing away and leaving those *keystone kops* behind, I clutched and floored it. They were relentless though and wouldn't quit. It didn't matter that my car was superior. I was wanted for *something*, though I didn't know what, and there was the matter of their pride being at stake as well. They would hunt me until they caught me and they wouldn't stop.

More shots came, but this time not as a diversionary tactic. No, this time they were shooting to kill. Fire rose like bile from the pit of my core with each thud that penetrated the *Audrey Manhattan*. Hot, white fury blazed through me for what they were doing. I could *kill* them, only I couldn't. It was forbidden. The police were untouchable. Any attack or offense against them could bring our entire underworld crashing down.

I pushed the *Manhattan* to her limits, forcing her to go faster, to outrun these bullets before any more struck home. I roared my car into the Theatre District in midtown, where the streets would be more populated, and Sciarra and his boys would have to be more cautious about flying bullets. Killing me could be justified by the untouchables, but not the accidental death of an innocent civilian. Collateral damage was unacceptable. I would use this as my shield.

The lights were bright in the Theatre District, millions of glistening bulbs from opera houses and movie theaters, restaurants and hotels, play houses and music halls. There weren't as many people out as I had hoped, but there were a couple pockets of transients about. They would have to do. I raced past a marquee that read *ICON* with the names of the actors starring in the show in gold lights below it, as I dodged in and out of the occasional car on the road. The bullets had stopped, but my pursuers were still there.

Had the traffic been heavier, I could have lost them in the crowd of cars. But because the amount of vehicles on the road was sparse and I had to weave my way around them, this was actually slowing me down rather than helping me vanish. And while I had to waste time and road and energy going around each vehicle, the civilians driving simply moved aside and opened a pathway for the police cars with their lights and sirens to get through, allowing them to get closer to me. Midtown just wasn't going to do. On to Plan B. Whatever Plan B was.

If I continued on my current trajectory, heading south, I would end up downtown. The Pro for being downtown was that there would certainly be more cars on the road and people about. The Con was downtown is where police headquarters was; which meant more cops at Sciarra's disposal to send after me and aid in their quest. Unless whatever Sciarra was up to was unlawful. He wouldn't risk getting other officers involved if what he was doing was illegal. But could I chance that?

My instincts told me *no*.

Avoiding downtown just in case seemed a wise and precautionary move. But where would I go? I couldn't keep the chase up forever. I was grateful to Cooper for keeping me gassed up, but even that wouldn't last. And I knew the man to be a genius when it came to automotive repair, I just prayed that his talents extended to bullet holes as well. My only hope was that the chase consisted of just the three of them and if I doubled back and started heading north again, or even east towards the water, that I would somehow lose them. Because I knew for a fact that they would not lose interest.

The bright and magical life of the Theatre District behind me, a sense of the normalcy of a city at night began to darken around me. Driving past Williams Square in the Washington Park section of town, a neighborhood notorious for crime and violence, I would use its natural guise and start to lose them here. The first alley I came across, I would sneak down and at the end would turn around and head elsewhere in the city.

One popped up and I turned, more concerned with my safety of getting away than the filth I was subjecting *Audrey* to in between the two corroded buildings on this trash laden throughway. The alley was long and thin, my Phantom only having inches on each side of the doors to the buildings closing me in. But then I saw the light. The light at the end of the tunnel. Sciarra hadn't come down the alley yet, but I was sure he had seen me go down it. It would only be a matter of time before he and his cohorts followed.

Speeding up as the exit grew closer, I needed to make sure that Sciarra and his boys didn't know which way I turned out of the end of the tunnel. Almost there. And that was when I was forced to slam on my brakes. Out of nowhere an obstruction pulled up, blocking the exit. The elongated body of a Chrysler Model B-70 patrol car parked itself across the outlet, directly blocking me.

Sciarra and his gang were all driving Packards. The Model B meant that someone new had joined the fray. There was no way out. I couldn't go forward and I didn't have enough time to reverse out of here. Any time now my three pursuers were going to turn down the front of that alley. I was boxed in.

Silk Stockings

Panic started to rocket through me. I was trapped. Desperately I searched around to see if there were any back doors to the dingy buildings, any means of escape or a way out. I saw nothing. Had this hunt been led by any other officer from the department other than Sciarra, now that I was caught I probably would have taken my chances with them and gone along quietly and figured out what this was all about. But not with Sciarra. Him I just did not trust.

I hated the final and only option presented me. I would have to blast my way out. The killing of police officers was forbidden, in any circumstance. And though something was amiss here, and what Sciarra and his goons were up to was probably illegal, in the end it would be my word against theirs. And I would not win; not against the Oldtowne police force, not in the eyes of society, and most importantly not with the Boss. This would bring too much heat too close to our operation. The Boss would not be forgiving, and I couldn't blame him.

But right now, only my survival instincts were kicking in. I removed the "Vest Pocket" from its holster and held it. Closing my eyes, I sighed deeply. Once the first bullet was shot and the firefight began, my life would forever change. *How the hell did this happen?*

Damnit!

I did a quick mental recap. There were no doors to escape through into the buildings. The alley was too far to reverse out of. A Model B-70 was blocking my exit. Exhaling slowly, I opened my eyes. I focused all my attention on the new patrol car in front of me. I could see the silhouette of a man inside but not who it was. The way I saw it, the only way out here was through. If I moved quickly enough and just fired warning shots at the newcomer, then maybe it would frighten him enough to get out of my way before Sciarra and the others showed up.

But then, the Model B moved of its own accord without any violent suggestions or threats from me. It backed up just enough to allow my Phantom passage out. Shaking off the confusion, I leapt at the opportunity and began to advance through. That's when the driver got out of the vehicle. Would he fire at me? He had me perfectly trapped. Was he just looking for legal justification to kill me as I passed? Fleeing the police in a moving vehicle is a felony; he could get away with my murder.

I braced myself for *anything* as I grew closer. And that's when I could make out the driver himself. *Paul…?* Ok so maybe I hadn't been prepared for *everything.*

Paul Caplan had been my partner on the force. I refused to believe that despite how much had changed in our country in the last five years that Paul would align himself with Sciarra.

"Hobbes!" I heard him exclaim.

I should ignore him and keep driving, get the hell out of there. But this was Paul. My partner. The man who I had trusted with my life for so many years. Maybe he knew what the hell was going on and why I had been targeted tonight. His weapon was not drawn I noticed.

Fuck.

I stopped the Phantom and he ran straight up to me and opened the drivers side door. I hoped that I wasn't going to regret this.

"Jon," Paul seemed exasperated. "Jon, there's no time to explain but we've gotta get you out of here."

"Paul what's going on?" I demanded.

He ignored me and started to physically remove me from the Phantom. "Take my patrol car and get out of here!" He ordered. Immediately I saw the wisdom in this. Paul would take the *Audrey Manhattan* while I could slip away in a police cruiser. He would be a diversion as Sciarra chased him through the streets. If they caught him, he was an officer of the law who had done nothing wrong. Proving that he had aided and abetted me would be difficult with no concrete evidence; it could have been Paul in the Phantom all along and never me. His word against theirs. And that was only if they caught him. If and when he got away, we could meet back up.

I had to think fast to set up a rendezvous point where we could reconnect safely and exchange cars. I knew precisely where to go. I gave him the address, we switched cars, and sped off in opposite directions.

She opened the door wearing a black bra and corset combination and a see-through chemise. Her dark hair was tousled; I had woken her. At 4AM she may have been the dreamer, but standing there in the doorway wearing very little between her and my imagination, she was every man's dream. Just looking at her brought back memories of the soft, naked body beneath that I sometimes got to enjoy. We had, after all, been occasional bedfellows.

"Hi Betty," I greeted, attempting to keep my eyes focused.

She stared right back at me nonplussed and unashamed of me seeing her nudity. Embarrassed, my eyes dropped, unable to hold her gaze. But of course my vision fell and focused on her supple legs. My eyes shot right back up.

"Jon?" She asked.

Overcoming the embodiment of sex standing before me, I got right on down to business. "Betty," I apologized, "I'm sorry. I had no place else to go."

Wordless, she nodded and ushered me in. Spending day in and day out together at the bar of the *Club,* and sometimes bed companions, there was probably no one on earth who knew me as well as Betty did. And in this moment, I was grateful for that. Poking her head out over the threshold of her door, she gave a quick once over up and down her corridor to ensure that no one was there. Then she shut and locked her door.

I was already in her living room and settling on her couch. I was taken aback by how comfortable I was in her house. She came and sat beside me, nestling her body into mine. No need for decency or pretense. Her peak-a-boo nakedness clearly didn't bother her so I wouldn't let it bother me.

"Are you ok Jon?" She asked with genuine concern. "What's going on?"

I didn't want to worry her with the details that the cops were after me, especially since I didn't know why. I just knew that I was in danger and had to lay low until this blew over. I also needed to forewarn her that at some point, hopefully sooner rather than later, that Paul would be coming here.

"My old partner will be meeting me here shortly," I informed her.

Tilting her head perplexed, she asked, "From when you were a cop."

I nodded assent, grateful that she let it go and didn't ask why. I'm sure we weren't the most opportune of gentleman callers.

She got up. "We're gonna need something to drink then, if I'm gonna have guests."

Betty moved to her bedroom to put on more clothes. Being nearly nude in front of me was one thing, but in front of another man she didn't know wouldn't be decent. She returned in long pants and long sleeved silver silk pajamas made of satin. Even covered I understood the contours of her body beneath her clothing. And a morsel of candy for the imagination were her hardened nipples piercing out from where they rubbed against the fabric.

My gaze followed her into the kitchen where two tumblers and a bottle of bathtub gin were already set out, as if she had known ahead of time that I was coming. Then looking more closely, I saw that one of the glasses had the glistening remains of ice chips at the bottom and the other was already stamped with cherry red lipstick. Maybe I hadn't woken Betty at all, perhaps she hadn't been asleep.

"We had some gin Rickey's," confirming that she hadn't been alone just a short while ago. "Want me to fix us some more?"

Lingerie... Tousled hair... Wow I felt stupid. I sincerely hoped I hadn't interrupted her late night date. "Umm, no," I didn't want her to go through the any trouble. "Just the gin is fine."

She poured the gin into a fresh tumbler for me, adding ice, then did the same in the glass she had already marked. Bringing the drinks over and returning to the spot she had chosen on the couch next to me, she must have clearly seen the flush of embarrassment in my reddened cheeks. Her smile as she handed me my cocktail became mischievous and flattered.

"Don't worry," she assured, "He's already gone." But she would say no more. And I didn't ask.

Clinking glasses and taking the gin into our mouths fulfilling the salutation, Betty smiled and then nestled herself into me, her head resting on my shoulder and snug against my neck.

Feeling the gin course through my veins and the warmth and comfort of Betty against me, this was the most peaceful I felt all day. This was a moment I wished could last forever. Sciarra was forgotten, my appointment with Nice Guy Eddie tomorrow night (tonight?) forgotten, even Eve was forgotten in the repose of Betty.

We drowsed together, each of us weary with the weight of our own evenings. Glasses were heavy in our hands, even as we emptied them. Eyes closed and succumbing to the coziness of the couch and one another.

The intrusion of the buzzer to her door snapped us back up.

It was Paul, I was sure if it. It had to be. But erring on the side of caution, I took out a gun, my body taught and alert. Wordlessly, I motioned for Betty to answer the door as I slid hidden into the background of her apartment. In the off chance that it *wasn't* Paul and indeed an enemy, they wouldn't know for sure that I was here. Add to that that I had positioned myself in a blind spot for whomever was at the door, I would have a momentary advantage that I would absolutely utilize.

Betty looked at me once more, wanting approval before opening the door. Nodding, I gave it.

"Who is it?" She asked before opening. Perfectly playing the part of a single woman who lived alone and was awoken at a licentious and improper time of the night.

"I'm here to see Hobbes," came the muffled voice of a man on the other side.

Again, Betty glanced at me for permission. I raised the gun higher so it was more direct. Betty opened the door. The man on the other side of the threshold was a stranger to Betty. I saw her body freeze. Still playing the part of a single woman alone at home, but faced with him, this time she wasn't acting. She was genuinely afraid.

Thank heaven it was unwarranted.

"Paul," I said, relieved, lowering my gun and stepping out of the shadows.

Betty stepped aside and let my old partner into her home, securing the door behind him. She then went to the kitchen to get Paul a drink and put on a pot of coffee.

"Been a long time," he remarked as we shook hands.

Betty came back into the room and handed Paul a glass of gin. For a split second it looked like he had been stung. He was looking at the liquid in the glass as if he had been handed poison.

"Been a long time for this too," he smirked, indicating the hooch. And then he drank gratefully.

Smiling, apparently amused by this awkward little reunion, Betty invited us to sit down at her small dining table. She busied herself in the kitchen preparing the coffee setup, as the joe percolated on the stovetop. Pretending to leave we men be to our conversation as she fussed with coffee cups and cream and sugar cubes, I knew Betty far too well to think she would simply ignore us. She lived for gossip. And some secret matter that involved the police was far too juicy for her to resist.

Paul and I stared at each other over our glasses of gin. I broke the silence, thanking him for saving my ass back there. I knew Paul was struggling with all this. He was in the apartment of some strange woman he didn't know if he could trust, his hands wrapped around a glass of bootleg home brew. Seeing me and getting himself involved with… whatever it was I was involved in. My old partner was a man who did things by the book. But he also had a Don't Ask, Don't Tell policy when it came to me. The department knew I was up to something but they weren't aware of precisely what I was doing. I was afforded some leniency due to the long tenure of my previous employment. Besides, just because imbibing alcohol was now illegal didn't mean that the boys in blue believed in it. They had just sworn to uphold the law. Ridiculous as it might be. At least my old partner didn't care that I couldn't adhere to it.

"Paul," I asked, "What's going on?"

By this time Betty had brought in the coffee and joined us. Her timing impeccable, and obvious, now that we were about to get into the meat and potatoes of it all.

Paul drained his glass before he would answer. It had probably been a long time since he had any liquid courage.

"I'm not really sure," he admitted. "But someone from high up wants you bad."

I was taken aback. "Who?"

Paul shook his head unknowingly. "I'm not sure, but whoever it is, they are important enough to get Commissioner Masterson out of bed and called down to the station."

My mind reeled at this information. *Who had that kind of power and authority? And why would they want* me? I had been wondering if this had to do with the murder of Eddie's driver somehow. Sciarra would love to nail me on a homicide charge. But no. No this went far above wasting energy on some low level thug from Atlantic City.

Could it be Enoch Johnson then? He certainly had the power and resources to wake a police Commissioner in the middle of the night. But why would he come after me? The driver had said that he and Eddie were undermining Johnson's authority and branching out on their own. Why send the cops after me then? It didn't make any sense. No, I think that if it had been Enoch Johnson that he would send his own men to take care of Nice Guy Eddie and his minions. I didn't think this was his doing. I was pretty certain I could rule him out.

What is going on then?

"So of course Sciarra volunteered to lead the manhunt," Paul continued. "Especially with Masterson on the warpath." Paul, of course, was also aware of the hard-on Sciarra had for me.

I didn't understand any of this. Who wanted me this badly? I couldn't shake the feeling that somehow Nice Guy Eddie was behind this. That he fit into this somewhere, somehow. Maybe he wasn't answering to Johnson anymore, but perhaps to someone else? This was the second time I got this feeling. He wasn't out all on his own as much as I was led to believe? Maybe it was this mysterious new benefactor who had interceded for him to get rid of me?

I name dropped Eddie to Paul to see how he would react.

"That maniac from Atlantic City?" He was genuinely surprised. "What would he be doing here in Oldtowne?"

So the Oldtowne police department did not know that Nice Guy Eddie was here operating in town. That cleared up the matter of the dead driver, but it didn't rule out Eddie having a superior other than Johnson.

"Doesn't matter," I replied. There was struggle in Paul's face. He wanted to know, badly, but he also knew that he probably *didn't* want to know. *Ask me no questions, I'll tell you no lies.*

He sat back, sipping on his coffee. A million unasked questions hanging in the air between us. And he was too polite to ask for another drink.

"So you came to Jon's rescue?" Betty interrupted, welcomingly, bringing the subject back to the story at hand.

"*Assistance*," I corrected. I was no damsel in distress. It came out harsher than I had intended, but it lightened the mood regardless as Paul and Betty started to laugh and I couldn't help but join in.

"Yea," Paul agreed, "I couldn't let Sciarra come after Jon when no facts were being offered by our superiors. I just didn't trust the situation."

I thanked him for coming after me and getting me out of the jam. And his idea of switching cars had been brilliant. Clearly he had shaken Sciarra and his goons off of his tail and came here to Betty's when it was safe to do so.

Neither of us had any more information to share. I hadn't been given much, but it was something. Someone out there who was powerful enough to wake a police commissioner wanted me out of commission. Could it be Eve's scorned lover? Was she connected with someone that high up in the food chain of power? Had he found out that she had come to my place tonight and sent the police after me as if they were his personal hit squad? Could someone actually be *that* jealous?

Whomever it was would have to wait for now. My plans hadn't changed, I still needed to face off with Nice Guy Eddie tonight at the Dual Peaks. I would just have to lay low until then and this mystery man would have to be out on hold for the time being.

Clearing his throat, Paul stood and excused himself. He needed to get home. His wife would know that his shift was long since over and would be worried. And everything written on the grimace on his face told me that he knew that when he arrived he would smell faintly of the perfume of a woman. *Betty's* perfume. Betty's perfume that acted like a magnet for men, intentionally or not, and would linger on his clothes like lipstick on a collar. Paul was such a good guy. By the book. He had risked his life, his job, and now even his marriage for me tonight.

I owed him more than I could ever repay.

Up with a Twist

What I had been dreading all day to do, was finally time to face. I was inside the parking garage of Betty's building, at the spot where Paul had left my Phantom. Inhaling deeply, I let out a sigh and braced myself for the damage. Several slugs had pierced my girl, defacing her. I slid a finger inside one of the puncture holes in the *Audrey Manhattan*, mourning and fury racing through me. Closing my eyes, I prayed that Earl Cooper was a holy man and could perform miracles with his hands.

Moving around to the driver's side of the vehicle, I could see the scratch wound on the wheel hood, still covered like blood in gunpowder residue and torn black paint, where a shot had ricocheted off of her. That cops had done this and there was nothing I could do but suck it up and take it infuriated me. Had this heinous act been committed by anyone else, they'd be dead already. But in our modern society of lawlessness, in order to keep business running smoothly the greatest sin was going against the police.

Right now there was nothing to be done. There was work to do. I would have to leave *Audrey* in this tarnished state until after the showdown with Eddie. Bringing the Rolls to life, I pulled her out of the garage, hit the freeway and made my way to the twin towers of the Dual Peaks hotel.

When I arrived I saw that Willie was on duty, as well as a full staff totaling four valets. Pulling into the portico of the valet station, Willie immediately came over to assist me. Valets were car lovers, it came with the territory, and it was hard not to admire my Phantom 1.

"Mr Hobbes," he greeted, opening the door for me.

I could tell that he was anxious to drive my car and I couldn't blame him. But instead I shook his hand, handing off the bill I had hidden in my palm.

"Good to see you, Willie," I told him. Then I discreetly said softly so that only he could hear, "Get someone else to take the car."

He understood that I wanted to deal with him and that he would be paid for it.

"Jake!" He called to another valet, who ran over immediately. "Take Mr.-" I shook my head, indicating for him to not use my name. "This Rolls to the parking deck," Willie recovered nicely. "And make sure not a speck of dust gets on it!" He then ordered.

"Yes sir," the valet named Jake accepted the assignment, climbed in my car and did as he was told.

"What can I do for you sir?" Willie asked once we were alone, and still not using my name.

"Has Nice Guy Eddie arrived yet?" I handed Willie another bill.

He accepted it without looking at it. "Not yet sir. Is he expected this evening?"

Willie and I moved to his work station podium, and he began filling me out a card for my car. From a distance it would appear as any other ordinary transaction with a customer who just dropped off his vehicle.

"He is," I told him, and then asked what his room number was. For another bill, he told me. "And his associate's room number?" I handed him more money and he gave me that as well.

When he had completed filling out the slip required to retrieve my vehicle, I tipped him; again, like an ordinary transaction. I then reached into my coat, purposely so that he could see the gun there, and retrieved another wad of cash that I gave him. Leaning in closely, I said, "And this is for all four of you to share. So that *no one* knows I'm here."

Willie took it appreciatively. And seeing the gun would remind him to not only pay his other three fellow workers, but that if I was betrayed in any way... well, I could certainly hand out more than just money.

Perhaps because of that or perhaps because I had paid him quite a large sum of money, Willie gave me a freebie. "The gentlemen you inquire about don't normally meet in their rooms however." He began to whisper as if divulging a secret of the universe, "They usually meet in the *Velvet Lounge.*"

The *Velvet Lounge.* I had heard of it, of course, but had never been. The Dual Peaks had its own Speakeasy and jazz lounge. Before Prohibition hit, the hotel had a fine dining restaurant, one of renown and best in the city. But on January 17th, 1920, when the Volstead Act took effect, they closed their heavy, wooden French doors. Seemingly for good. Whispers came shortly thereafter, in the hush-hush socialite circles of illicit dealings, that the Dual Peaks had opened a new concept called the *Velvet Lounge;* a club only for elite clientele.

It made sense that Eddie and his driver would meet here. It was public, so they would both feel safe, though illegal and therefore guarded and secluded. They could conduct their business in private and not have to worry about their rooms being watched or any betrayal from one another.

Willie was a shrewd one. He gave me this nugget of information for free, but the daily password and the location of the entrance I would certainly have to pay for. Admiring his cleverness and his aptitude for greed, I complied with more greenbacks.

"Blue," he informed me of the password and told me how to get there.

"Martini," I ordered, "With a twist." And then thinking of my early morning cocktails with Betty, I added, "And not some bullshit bathtub gin. Give me something good."

The *Velvet Lounge* was small. Dark and intimate. Apparently it had received its name from the fabric that covered all of the chairs, chaise lounges and even the walls; it was all adorned in soft velvet. A sole candle on each of the small, round tables littered about the room were the only sources of light, save for the hazy red spotlight that lit the stage for whichever crooner or siren was offering throaty renditions of torch songs.

I had chosen a martini for two distinct reasons. Rather than my preferred inclination toward whiskey, the martini seemed more appropriate for the room. It was like camouflage, a veil to hide behind, helping me to blend in with the scenery and other patrons. And secondly, I just needed a drink. The vest and bow tied gentleman behind the bar did not fill the crystalline mixer with vermouth and gin to stir them, but rather poured the ingredients in a shaker over ice. Shaking the tin vigorously, the liquid inside slamming around the rocks of ice, he bruised the gin so that when it was poured into the coupe before me there would be cool and clean ice chips forming on the top layer of liquid.

Immersing myself further into the atmosphere of the *Lounge*, I took my cocktail and sat at a table, choosing one with the best vantage point to observe the room for when Eddie came in. The view to the bar and to the main entrance were direct and unobstructed, I was a casual observer who had the full panorama of the lounge. I would have much rather stood at the bar to enjoy my drink, but this wasn't a social call it was work. For a moment I considered extinguishing the candle flame on my table so that I could view the room better without being seen, hidden in the shadowed darkness of my little enclave in the room. But then I thought better of it; I didn't want to draw undue attention in my direction by being the sole table without a flame. Eddie was not a stupid man and I didn't want to draw his suspicions.

That first sip of the martini, the ice crystals gathering on my lip, was cold and refreshing. I was discreet with my glances around, not being obvious. I was just another patron, privileged enough to be allowed access into the *Velvet Lounge*, hidden in plain sight. Exactly like the *Lounge* itself. When their fancy restaurant closed, the Dual Peaks had barred their double doors into the restaurant not just with lock and key but also with a great chain, sealing it off forever like some tomb of a forgotten time. Inside however, they had gone to work. Leaving the dining room as it was, a relic just beyond the great doors, (and a cover should any unwanted authorities actually make it through the main doors), they completely converted the small kitchen in the back into the fashionable and elegant *Velvet Lounge* of today. And the only way in was through a service elevator that had originally led to the back of the kitchen for deliveries, an elevator that was, for all intents and purposes, defunct and out-of-order to the general public and defenders of the law and guarded by a daily changing password.

At the end of a short corridor leading in and out of the *Velvet Lounge*, the service elevator doors slid open. A single dim bulb was inside so as to not intrude bright light into the ambiance of the *Lounge*. Two men were in the lift I saw once the doors were completely retracted. The first man was the beefy elevator attendant, who was the same build and had the same function as Happy and Harry the Cat. I had given him the *Blue* password just a short while ago to get access in here. The other man made my body tense and my blood run colder than the martini before me.

It was Nice Guy Eddie.

This was it. The reckoning was here.

Eddie walked in, scanning the room as he did so. I put my face down into my glass so he couldn't get a good look at me. Besides, it was dark in here and I wasn't the man he was expecting to see or looking for. And if it had been he who had somehow orchestrated Commissioner Masterson sending Sciarra after me last night, he probably thought I was either in police custody or dead.

He stood at the bar, in pretty much the same exact spot I had just a short while ago. Some Belle Baker imitator took to the stage and beneath a hazy spotlight began her fiery lament. I had a clean shot at him from sitting right here at my table. I could end this, end *him*, right now and he would die never the wiser. But if I were to kill him now, my actions would be seen by the other patrons in the bar and misconstrued and I probably wouldn't make it out of here without having to blast my way out, which was unacceptable and would not do. No, I had to lure Eddie out of here and get him alone; which would be tricky. Besides, I had my pride to consider. I wanted him to know that it was me. That in the end I beat him. That although he had been winning the small battles along the way in our cat-and-mouse tête-à-tête, when all was said and done I had won the war.

He ordered a drink, I didn't hear what. And as he sipped it, he tried to appear casual but there was a nervousness about him as he fidgeted here and there. His eyes constantly roamed over to where the elevator doors would open up into the *Lounge.* He awaited his accomplice, his driver, anxiously. Perhaps Eddie was naturally a nervous man? Or maybe he had expected his driver to already be here waiting for him? It was the subordinate's job to wait, after all.

Taking advantage of his distraction of turning his head to peer at the entrance, I nonchalantly moved towards the bar as if to order another drink or pay my tab; but behind his line of vision. Far enough away from him to be casual and not startle him, but still close enough where I could pounce on him. The bartender moved down the bar toward me to see to my needs, perfectly normal behavior. Eddie gave a quick glance at the movement of the bar man, but resumed his focus on the door almost immediately. He didn't see me coming. And just as the barkeep opened his mouth to see how he could assist me, I was on Eddie from behind, my .45 pressed into his side. He was startled, but was enough of a professional to know what was digging in his rib cage so he didn't resist.

"Put my drinks on his tab," I told the bartender, who was also alarmed by my sudden movement. Only he wasn't quite sure what was going on; he couldn't see the gun I held against Eddie. For all he knew we could be two old friends whose balls I was breaking by coming up on him like this.

To Eddie I said, "I've got you now, you *sonofabitch*." And with that, he knew it was me who had him.

In the dusty mausoleum of the old dining room, everything was still intact and set, as if ready for dinner service when the doors opened. Except the white table clothes were now soiled and dirty. Layers of dust had settled on top of layers of dust on the china and flatware. Cobwebs strung from glass to glass. It was quite the juxtaposition, exiting the sultry dark and intimate lounge and into the haunting and ghostly dining room where I had threateningly led Nice Guy Eddie with my M1911.

Eddie was silent as I brought him into the empty room. It seemed fitting that he should die here, I thought, as the room itself looked like a graveyard already. No one in the lounge had been the wiser when I had taken Eddie in here, having done it without any fuss or ruckus. Maybe the bartender suspected something, but I would have to chance that. As for Eddie himself, I had to hand it to him, he was coming along quietly and without struggle. How many times had he been in my shoes in this same kind of situation? He knew it was useless to struggle or resist. If nothing else, he was a professional til the last.

"It never had to be this way," I told him. "Oldtowne has always gotten along well with Atlantic City; our interests never conflicted." He was about to die and I was about to kill him and I wanted him to know that whatever it was he was doing here was useless.

He didn't respond.

Perhaps a more direct question then. "Why are you here?" Eddie turned to look at me, his hard eyes cold and full of hate. Still he said nothing. *Fuck you, buddy.* Maniac and monster though he may be, I was not afraid of him. Now he was just aggravating me. Squeezing my grip on his arm tighter and pressing the gun harder into his side, I demanded, "What is your objective here?"

The malice in his face softened into something like amusement. He knew he was getting to me. Even now, under my thumb and in my control, he still had something over on me. Because my blood was starting to boil and wisps of anger were starting to rise in me while he remained calm and collected, he was winning. He was beating me. Still.

Fine. I was getting sick of this fucking game. If he didn't want to give me any answers then I would just kill him without learning any.

"The wine was a trophy," he told me tauntingly, changing the subject. Buying time.

It worked.

My interest was piqued. "But not for you." It wasn't a question.

He was still amused, a sardonic smile on his face. Even more amused now than a moment ago when he realized he was getting under my skin.

"No," he agreed, "Not for me."

So he *had* stolen the Domaine Romanée-Conti for someone else. But was he paid to do it by some fellow underworld associate or was this just more evidence that he was working for someone else who had sent him here to Oldtowne? My guess was the latter.

Eddie was stalling, saying only just enough to keep my trigger finger at bay. Maybe he was waiting for his partner, his driver, to show up to their meeting and look for him in here. *Sorry Eddie.* All he really was doing however was annoy me.

When he had brought up the wine, my tension on his arm loosened. I had wanted to hear what he'd say. Now that I knew that he wasn't going to give me anything concrete, I was through playing this game and I wasn't going to let him purchase one more second. I didn't retighten the grip I had on him nor press the gun any harder. But with it I did nudge him along with it. I wanted to get him into an open clearing in the center of the room to have more space to execute him. All amusement vanished from his face. Eddie knew I wasn't playing anymore, he knew this was it. And he realized that his driver wouldn't get here in time to help him, and I knew that his driver would never come at all.

This was when he struck. A desperate last ditch attempt by a dead man walking. He rushed his arm up, freeing from the hold I had on him, and his elbow crashed into my face. It was a dangerous move on his part, my gun was still in his side and all I needed to do was shoot. But he knew he had to try something, he was dead either way.

His action worked. A light exploded in my head when his elbow cracked into my nose and face. He didn't break anything, but the pain was searing and caused my vision to momentarily go. If I did shoot, I would be firing blind. Literally. Echoing my words from mere moments ago, "Son of a bitch!"

Eddie used these moments of my incapacitation to get away. He bolted towards the front of the restaurant to the great double doors. They were heavy, massive and ornate, custom crafted fleur-de-lis carved into the wood. Here Eddie made his first mistake. On the other side of those doors, viewed from the public, was a large golden decorative and symbolic chain barring the doors from opening. But on this side, was a real chain that locked the doors so that no one could get out or *in*.

My vision and my senses were returning by this point, though lightheaded and not one hundred percent, and I began shooting. Eddie was far enough away from me and a target on the move that he evaded my shots and retrieved his own weapon from an ankle holster and began shooting back. Diving for cover as cobwebbed wine glasses shattered about me, Eddie used this opportunity to double back away from the French doors and started back towards the *Velvet Lounge*, his only way out. From the ground, I started shooting between table legs at his running feet; with no luck.

I stayed down as he fired wildly back at me without turning around, focused ahead on where he was going. No way did I want to be hit by a stray bullet. Once out of the dining room, I got up and went after him, changing the clip in my gun. Hopefully I'd be able to corner him inside the *Velvet Lounge,* he'd be much more difficult to catch once free out and about in the hotel.

It took a moment for my eyes to adjust back to the darkness of the *Lounge* from the ghostly grey of the dining room. Eddie was on the far side of the room, heading down the short corridor and still moving fast. The elevator doors were already opened before he even got there. Did this fucking guy have a four-leaf-clover as a boutonnière? He was always so goddamn lucky!

I called out to the attendant to stop him, not let him get away, my voice an intrusion in the hushed intimacy of the *Lounge*; attracting the attention of the customers trying to enjoy themselves. I didn't care. The elevator attendant's head snapped up in awareness and saw Eddie coming towards him. But Eddie's bullets were faster than the reflexes of the bouncer or my words. Nice Guy Eddie fired twice, putting two plugs into him. The elevator doors had closed by the time I reached it and the lift was on the move. I banged my fist on the sealed door in frustration.

The floor indicator had been dismantled, purposely, so I had no idea in which direction Eddie was taking the elevator. Up or down? Down would give him access out of the hotel, but someone in the loading dock where this elevator exited would be sure to see a dead man in the lift. Up would get Eddie back of house access to the floor he and his driver had rooms on. And given that his driver never showed up to the meeting, it was my guess that that was the direction he was heading.

If Eddie was doing as I surmised and heading for reinforcements in the driver, he would jam the elevator so it wouldn't come back down and hide the body of the attendant in some cursory manner. I asked the bartender curtly where the back stairwell was. Eyes never leaving the gun in my hand, he told me. I found it easy enough and made my way up to the floor both Eddie and his driver had rooms on, taking stairs two and three at a time.

After ten floors of running, I arrived on the twentieth floor. Eddie's floor. I took a breath before I exited the stairwell to collect myself. Caution was needed now; I wasn't sure precisely where Eddie would be. The stairwell emptied out into a storeroom of some kind, stacks and rows of extra folding chairs and round tables used for large functions lined everywhere. The back of house behind the scenes interior of the hotel wasn't nearly as luxurious as the public areas of the hotel. Slowly I made my way through the cluttered corridors of the inner workings of the hotel, careful to not disturb anything or make noise. In the *Velvet Lounge* I had the element of surprise over Eddie. That was blown now and I needed to be as covert as possible.

Room 2001, the drivers room, was in the middle of the corridor down on my right as I exited the service door of the inner workings of the hotel and into the more posh hospitable area of the Dual Peaks. My timing getting there was impeccable, because Nice Guy Eddie was only now escalating his knock on the door to a harder rapt. It must have taken him this time to stall the elevator and hide the body he had eliminated. We had arrived here at just about the same time, he only mere heartbeats ahead of me. He wouldn't get an answer, I knew, because I had left the driver beneath a layer of hay at the racetrack. Even now, Eddie did not know that.

Once I stepped out into the hallway, he would see me in his peripheral and know I was there. Killing him from here would be difficult and he would abandon his attempt at raising his driver's attention. Slowly, I stepped out of the service door and into the hallway. I began raising my gun in the most lackadaisical fashion, as to not draw any more attention.

Eddie saw anyway.

And instead of taking off down the corridor as I expected, he kicked in the hotel room 2001 door and dove in. Out of the line of fire, I had no choice but go after him. As I advanced, my professional training noticed something. No light had issued out of 2001. No light spilled out into the hallway with the the forced opening of the door. Which meant that all the lights had been off, making perfect sense to me as the driver left for the track during the day and hadn't needed the lights on. It also meant that clearly, to Eddie, the driver wasn't in there right now.

"He's already dead," I shouted to Eddie as I ran up the hall. I hoped this news would hit him like a bullet and incapacitate him some. "I saw him die," I assured, hoping this would take him off his guard and give me an advantage.

Whether he believed me or not didn't matter at this point, because either way no one was in the room now, no one who could help. I think Eddie believed me too, for I had no reason to lie. And even if I did, it didn't refute the fact that the driver didn't show up to their prearranged meeting and that he also wasn't here now. Eddie was surprised, unpleasantly.

His answer to all of this was to fire at me.

I slammed my loping body against the wall to avoid the bullets. It bought him the time he needed to get out of the driver's room with the now broken door. Eddie zig zagged all the way up the hall while still firing back at me to keep distance. I knew he didn't have very far to go. His room was only a handful of doors up at 2010. But he was firing blindly at me and I was firing only sporadically back at him. This was a stalemate that I did not fancy. I was pissed at myself for losing the edge I had earlier.

Eddie made it to his room, inserted the key and rushed inside. I made it there just as he secured the door; hotel doors locking themselves automatically. *Fuck this guy.* I put a bullet into the door handle, blasting the lock and knob right off.

This time light did spill out into the hallway, me engulfed in it. I stood on the threshold, looking for Eddie. I wanted to kill him. I needed to kill him. Oldtowne was my home and I had to protect it from thieves and monsters, gangsters like Nice Guy Eddie. However, standing there in the doorway, it was my turn to be surprised, unpleasantly. From the hallway looking into the room, I may not have seen Nice Guy Eddie but I did see… Eve.

Eve?

Her legs dangled over the edge of the bed, and her form was draped over itself; her head resting in her palms, while her elbows dug into her knees. A cigarette burning unsmoked held between her fingers. She was a semi-crumpled version of herself. A million thoughts raced through my head. *What the fuck? Why was she here? Why did she look so deflated?* My arms fell to my side as I looked in at her, the .45 included. Trying to place her. Figure out her role in all of this. Why she was in Nice Guy Eddie's hotel room?

Eddie himself used this to his advantage. As he spun out of the washroom and advanced like a bull towards me, my body didn't react as quickly as my brain that I was caught more off guard of Eve being here than Eddie was. She was sitting up now and screaming, her body a rigid form. At me? At him? Everything seemed to be happening in slow motion. Eddie didn't get a shot off at me and my gun was still by my side, as he slammed into me, shouldering himself into my body hard enough to bring me to the carpet and he kept going.

Even on the floor I did not understand. Eve…?

It was then, sitting there, that a million things fell into place. A million things of logic that fought against the emotion in my brain. Of course Eve was here. And of course this was the place that Eve ran off to after she left my apartment and I chased her. She didn't belong to me, she never did. She belonged to Nice Guy Eddie. I was just fool enough to think she was mine. She was the reason why Nice Guy Eddie had been one step ahead of me the entire time.

She was still on the edge of the bed, just standing up when I raised my gun. And pointed it at her. She just looked at me, wordless, and the both of us knew. I could kill her. Eve. This incredible creature. My *Sensation.*

Eddie was gone down the hallway, gaining more distance. But I didn't care. I looked at her and she at me. She at *me* and not my gun pointed at her. All I had to do was squeeze. But I didn't, couldn't. After what seemed an eternity and the frustration of my inability to act, I huffed and took off after Eddie. He was the priority here. Not Eve.

Fucking Eve.

The greatest piece of ass and the first woman I could see giving myself to since Rosaline, my ex wife. She was just the right combination of beautiful, erotic and mysterious. She could drink like me. And she could be accepting and unafraid of my... occupation. Of course she could. She was a spy in my bed. And I had fallen for it.

Bitch.

Midway up the long hallway of the twentieth floor, Eddie banked left through a glass door. It was the entranceway to the sky bridge. If he made it to the other tower, he had a better chance of losing me and getting away. I had to stop him there.

Heartbeats later I too went through the glass door and came onto the sky bridge. The bridge connecting the two towers of the Dual Peaks hotel was like a luxurious concrete train car in shape with floor to ceiling tall round-arched windows. The view from this height was spectacular, which I didn't have the time to enjoy at the moment. Eddie was about three quarters to the other side. I fired a warning shot beside him, blowing out one of the great windows. Air rushed in like the snap of a whip. And it got the response from Eddie that I intended. He halted. I didn't want a moving target; stationary was so much easier.

He turned to face me, slowly. Arms just over his head, gun in one hand. While mine was trained on him, he said, "You're wrong, Hobbes, it always had to be this way."

It took me a moment to realize he was referring back to my original question from back down in the dining room, when I had informed him that it didn't need to be this way. So *now* he wanted to talk. But I wasn't going to let him talk his way out of this.

"You're out of your league, Hobbes." That sardonic smile back. "This is just the beginning," he spat.

"Toss the weapon!" I ignored him.

For a second, he ignored my command. Contemplating his position. But then he thought better of it and did as I said.

"Oldtowne will go down in flames and your city will be ruins." His words were his weapon now; the only one left to him.

"Not by you, Eddie."

"No," he agreed with a short laugh of contempt. "Not by me. I was only to get Oldtowne ready, get her ripe for the taking."

My hands tightened around the .45. "For who?"

He smiled. The damned man actually smiled. His continuous amusement was infuriating.

"My new employer, of course." His smile grew and on a man like him, it was harsh and mischievous. "He's going to enjoy that red wine I stole for him. But not as much as when your streets run red with blood."

"What's his name?" I demanded.

There was actual joy on his face. He was enjoying this.

"His name? His name is Mr.-"

BLAM! BLAM!

In rapid succession two shots were fired from behind me, tearing into Nice Guy Eddie. Sending him reeling back. His body slammed into the rail by the window I had blown out. Spinning to face this new adversary, Eve stood there, legs apart and both hands wrapped around a smoking gun.

"Eve!" I called.

She ignored me. I knew Eddie was dead by the time he had hit the railing, but before his body could slump to the ground, Eve fired more bullets into him, the impacts of which forced his body over the rail and out the shattered window. I ran to the closest window to see this. There was too much disbelief in a handful of seconds. Eddie's bullet-ridden and lifeless body cascading down story after story at a sickening rate.

I didn't wait for the final crash. I didn't want to see it. Turning back, I faced Eve. Who was now pointing her gun at me.

"I had to kill him, Jon," she tried to rationalize herself with me. With the gun, she was keeping distance between us. "I had to kill that son of a bitch." Despite the precariousness of the situation, I couldn't help but find it humorous that the both of us referred to Eddie that way.

"Lower the gun, Eve," I pleaded. Perhaps she was on my side after all. Playing the double agent had been too much for her. And in the end it was me who she had chosen, over him.

My hands were held up before me, in a non threatening manner. To ease her fears. Tears were flowing silently down her bruised face. Her mascara ruined and running. One of her eyes half shut and purple from where she had been struck. She did not lower the gun.

"He hit me," she told me, her voice stoic and her expression blank. "That son of a bitch hit me. His plans were falling apart and he lashed out in his anger." She was speaking aloud, but it was more to herself than an explanation to me. "At *me*."

There was a sudden change in her body language, I saw it. Her stance became focused. Something was going through her mind and it showed all over her face. Whatever it was, a decision had been reached. I understood her pain. That a powerful man, a man like Nice Guy Eddie, had used his anger and considerable strength on one such as she. I would need to reason with her. Help her understand that it was over now. The nightmare complete.

Eve fired the gun once more. My entire life flashed before me. The sound was deafening and final. She hadn't chosen me. But she hadn't chosen Eddie either. In the end, Eve had chosen herself. She had fired the gun. But at the last second she pulled her arm to the right, her bullet smashing the window out, just I had done to the other, shards of glass blowing back and then down to the earth below.

I stared at her, horror struck. Grateful that I was alive. Disbelief at what she had done, but grateful that she had decided not to shoot at me. She was in some kind of shock. Her mannerisms and the way she moved her body seemed not her own. The gun went limp at her side and she let it go, clinking against the concrete. She looked at me once more, her tear-lined face blank. For the smallest second there was some kind of emotion in her eyes, some recognition. And then like a *poof* it was gone.

That was when she charged towards the empty window and threw herself out.

"NO!" I screamed, reacting, and lunged for her. I got ahold of her arm, but all it did was twist her around. My hold wasn't a good one, as I had been caught off guard. She had been going too fast and I lost my grip. This couldn't be happening, shouldn't be happening. She had made it past me. I had my hand on her and I fucking lost it. Instead of head first out, she was now falling with her back to the ground. And able to look back up at me as she screamed. We watched each other as she fell. *Now* there was understanding and life in her eyes.

Her scream grew silent as she flailed. I didn't see Eddie's drop to its conclusion, but Eve I had to see through until the end.

"*Eve…*" I whimpered.

Eve was gone.

Digestif

The flame of the torch ignited the red embers of my cigar, the brown leaf wrapper blackening as it started to burn. I inhaled on it deeply to get the stick going. Puffs of smoke billowed away from me.

I was alone at the long board table of the Boss' suite. The two way mirror across from me still dark. The Boss may have summoned me up here, but as always, we were on his time table. At least I had company while I waited. He had provided me with this cigar and an etched crystalline decanter filled with brandy. Removing the crystal bulb stopper, I poured the liquid in the tumbler and took a healthy sip. I smiled appreciatively, it was Armagnac. Combined, the two were a perfect pair, and I indulged in both appreciatively.

"Jon," the Boss announced his presence at last. I was still in the first third of the cigar but the bottom third of the elixir in the glass. I deserved it.

Topping myself off with the Armagnac, I began filling in the Boss the details of the rest of the story, starting with finding Eve in my bed last night before she had run off and all the way through to the events on the sky bridge. Not a single detail was missed or omitted. There was silence on the other side of that mirror, the Boss taking it all in.

When I finished the tale, he told me that he had finally gotten through to Enoch Johnson in Atlantic City. He learned straight from Johnson of Nice Guy Eddie's defection and subsequent going awol. Unfortunately he had no more information than that. But Johnson has assured the Boss that desertion from his organization was a crime punishable by death, especially from a Capo; they knew too much. If Nice Guy Eddie so much as showed hair or hide in New Jersey again, he would assuredly be dealt with in the strictest sense. Not that it mattered any longer.

Together we started piecing everything together. Eddie had deserted his post and affiliation with Enoch Johnson and aligned himself with someone new, a powerful mystery man who had laid his sights on Oldtowne for some reason. A man powerful enough to have influence over the Oldtowne police department and send them after me to impede my actions. Eddie was going to reveal his name to me. He *wanted* me to know who was coming. Eve had ruined that opportunity and the words died on Eddie's lips, literally. Eve, who had been feeding the late Nice Guy Eddie with information of my every move. Our pillow talk and conversations. And god knows what other intimate details. She had been tasked to infiltrate my life and she had done a damn good job. And after every encounter, she reported her findings back to Nice Guy Eddie. I was only a mark to her and she had used her sex as her weapon, her greatest weapon.

Eve…

The question of what had happened to the Boss' DRC was now answered as well. It was now in the possession of Eddie's employer. We also concluded that the charade with the milk truck had been a diversion, a misdirection to whatever was really going on. Also, Eve had said that Eddie's plans were falling apart and that was what had triggered his anger and subsequent abuse. From my point of view, he had been one step ahead of me the entire time. And he hadn't known of the murder of his accomplice until he had reached his dark and empty room during the chase in the hotel. So what had happened? Was he not up to date on whatever timetable had been set? Were there tasks he was supposed to have fulfilled but hadn't yet? It didn't matter anymore. If Eddie had been behind, that only would work to our advantage. Especially now that he would never be able to fulfill his obligations here in Oldtowne.

We would need to find out the identity of Eddie's employer, of course, but that could hold for now. The only real lead we could follow at the moment lied in the upper hierarchy of the police department, an avenue I would not be able to pursue. Maybe Paul could investigate and find out more, but I was reluctant to put him out any more than I already had. Besides, I had the feeling that whoever it was that wanted Oldtowne wouldn't stop just because Nice Guy Eddie was dead. No, he would invoke a contingency plan of some kind and make another move against us. We just had to be ready.

The briefing with the Boss adjourned, I returned downstairs. Betty was there waiting for me, tray in hand with two glasses on it. A smile on her face and a smile in her liquid brown eyes. Setting the tray down on the corner edge of the bar, she picked up one of the glasses and handed it to me. I took it gratefully while she took the other.

"To?" I asked as we clinked glasses.

"Don't say it," she requested and drained the contents of her glass and scurried away to make her rounds of the *Ace of Clubs*.

To Eve, I obeyed, not saying her name aloud. I took a long look at the liquid in the glass knowing this would be the final act for Eve the Sensation I would ever commit for her again. I downed the shot, forgetting her, and got back to my post behind the bar and got back to work.

The night proved to be a busy one. Good for business and my pocket. But during the intermittent calm times I thought often of this mystery employer.

"Mr... ECK-"

Eddie was only getting out the beginning of the first syllable of the name when Eve shot him full of holes. There was no telling what the name could have been.

Mr. and then *ECK* – the sound his body made as the bullet slammed into him and killed him. Any chance of discovering what the name had been disappeared in Eddie's final, gurgling breath. *Mr.* and then *ECK*. It was nothing to go on.

Mr. ECK.

This was just the beginning. Eddie had only been the front man, the precursor. The real threat was still out there. And he was coming.

I would have to find him. And I would have to kill him. This mystery boss pulling the strings. This faceless villain who wanted to move in on Oldtowne. This nameless enemy who was out there somewhere, in the shadows. This Mr.... *ECK.*

This Mr. X.

Finis

Jon Hobbes Will Return

Lexicon

Whiskey or (Whisky)
Distilled alcoholic spirit. Brown liquid.
Made from fermented grain mash. Various grains, which may be malted, are used for different varieties, including barley, corn, rye, and wheat.
Strictly regulated worldwide. Various types and classes.

Bourbon
Distilled alcoholic spirit. Brown liquid.
Type of whiskey.
American whiskey, barrel aged, made from a corn based mash. Name derived from the
French Bourbon dynasty.

Rye
Distilled alcoholic spirit. Brown liquid.
Type of whiskey.
Spicier, drier, more austere than bourbon. Not as full bodied.
By United States law, American rye whiskey must be made from a mash of at least 51 percent rye. Other ingredients of the mash are usually corn and malted barley.

Gin
Distilled alcoholic spirit. Clear liquid.
Evolved from an herbal medicine, a diverse botanical spirit.
Most common ingredient and predominant flavor comes from juniper berries.
Based on jenever, an old Dutch liquor.

Champagne

French sparkling wine deriving from
Champagne region of northern France, ninety miles
north of Paris.
Primary grape varietals are Pinot Noir, Chardonnay
and Pinot Meunière.
Must undergo a secondary fermentation in the bottle
to create carbonation.

Cognac

Distilled alcoholic spirit. Brown liquid.
Type of brandy.
From the village of Cognac in western France.
A type of brandy or *eau de vie* (water of life)
produced in
pot stills by double distilling
and aging white wine for a minimum of two years
in aged Limousin oak casks.

Vodka

Distilled alcoholic spirit. Clear liquid.
Of Russian or Polish origin.
Composed primarily of water and ethanol, but
sometimes with traces of impurities and flavorings.
Traditionally, vodka is made through the distillation
of cereal grains, rye, wheat or potatoes that have
been fermented, though some modern technique use
fruits or sugar.

Scotch

Distilled alcoholic spirit. Brown liquid.
Type of whiskey made in Scotland.
Made from malted barley, wheat or rye and must be
aged in oak barrels for a minimum of three years.
Classified into five distinct categories: single malt
Scotch whisky, single grain Scotch whisky, blended
malt Scotch whisky, blended grain Scotch whisky
and blended Scotch whisky.

First Growth Bordeaux

Classification system of wines primarily for the Bordeaux region of France.

From the French *Premier Cru*.

Emperor Napoleon III requested a classification system for the best Bordeaux wines for the *Exposition Universelle of 1855* which resulted in the Bordeaux Wine Official Classification of 1855.

The highest ranked wines were named the *Grand Crus Classés* or Great Classified Growths.

Brandy

Distilled alcoholic spirit.

Eau de vie (water of life).

Produced by distilling wine or pomace.

Madiera

Fortified wine made on the Madeira Islands of Portugal.

Classified into four categories, ranging fry dry to syrupy sweet: Sercial, Verdelho, Bual and Malvasia.

Sercial

A white grape grown in Portugal, especially on the island of Madeira. The driest style of the four classic varieties of Madeira fortified wine.

Domaine de la Romanée-Conti

An estate in Burgundy, France that produces Pinot Noir and Chardonnay.

Regarded as one of the world's greatest and most expensive wine producers.

Taking its name from the domaine's most famous vineyard, Romanèe-Conti, and is often abbreviated to DRC.

Domaine de la Romanèe-Conti vintage 1923

1900 to 1945

In the 20th century, there wasn't any exceptional vintages before 1911, offering wines with remarkable longevity and followed a few years later by the 1915. Burgundy also experienced a good series in the 1920s, with three exceptional vintages: 1920, 1923 and 1929. The 1920 and 1923 vintages are still good today, but they are very rare, since the harvest was exceptionally small. 1929 was probably the best year of the decade, with very good tannin structures and aging potential.

Taittinger Blanc de Blanc

Taittinger is the family name of one of the most famous Champagne houses.

Blanc de Blanc is from the French White of White, meaning that this particular champagne is 100 percent Chardonnay.

Vermouth

Originally produced in Turin, Italy.

An aromatized, fortified wine flavored with roots, spices, herbs, barks and other botanicals.

Classified into two categories: dry (blanc) and sweet (rosso).

Digestif

An alcoholic beverage, usually served neat, served after a meal to aid with digestion.

Armagnac

Distilled alcoholic spirit. Brown liquid.

Type of brandy.

Produced in southwest France, in the Armagnac region of Gascony.

Distilled from a blend of grapes traditionally using a column still and aged in oak barrels.

Cocktail Menu

Champagne cocktail

In a champagne flute place a sugar cube
Add 3 dashes of Angostura Bitters onto the cube
Splash just under half an ounce of brandy (preferably cognac)
Fill flute with champagne
Garnish with a lemon twist and brandy-soaked griotte cherries

Old Fashioned

In it's namesake glass, an Old Fashioned glass (tumbler), muddle together a sugar cube, two brandy-soaked griotte cherries and an orange slice (careful to only crush the flesh of the orange, not the rind)
Add a drop of water
Add a large format ice cube or fill the glass with regular ice cubes (as desired)
Pour 2 ounces of whiskey (generally rye or bourbon)

Sidecar*

In a shaker fulled with ice, combine:
2 ounces of Cognac
¾ ounce of an orange liqueur (ie a triple sec, Cointreau, Grand Marnier, Dry Curaçao, etc)
¾ ounce of fresh squeezed lemon
¾ ounce simple syrup
Shake and strain into a coupe or a martini glass
Garnish with a lemon twist

French 75*

In a shaker filled with ice, combine:
1.5 ounces of gin
¾ ounce fresh squeezed lemon
¾ ounce simple syrup
Shake and strain into a coupe, martini glass or champagne flute
Garnish with a lemon twist
Top with champagne

* Legend has it that both the Sidecar and the French 75, and also the Bloody Mary, were all invented just after World War I at *Harry's Bar New York* in Paris, France.

As a pop cultural reference, *Harry's Bar New York* was mentioned in the 1960 short story *From a View to a Kill* by Ian Fleming in which his titular character James Bond recalls his first visit to Paris at 16 years old. And after an evening of revelry at *Harry's*, James goes on that night to lose his virginity.

Gimlet

In a shaker filled with ice, combine:
2 ounces of gin
1 ounce fresh squeezed lime juice
½ ounce simple syrup
Shake and strain into a martini glass or serve on the rocks
Add a splash of club soda
Garnish with a lime wheel

Bees Knees

In a shaker filled with ice, combine:
2 ounces of gin
¾ ounce fresh squeezed lemon
¾ ounce honey
Shake and strain into a coupe or a martini glass
Garnish with a lemon twist

The Last Word

In a shaker filled with ice, combine:
1 ounce gin
1 ounce green chartreuse
1 ounce Maraschino liqueur
1 ounce fresh squeezed lime
Shake and strain into a coupe or a martini glass
Garnish with a lime twist and brandy-soaked griotte cherries

Ward 8

In a shaker filled with ice, combine:
2 ounces of rye whiskey
½ ounce fresh squeezed lemon
½ ounce fresh squeezed orange
½ ounce grenadine*
Shake and strain into a chilled rocks glass
Served neat
Garnish with an orange twist and brandy-soaked griotte cherries
(or the flag of Boston, MA)

* Grenadine is a pomegranate based, sweet and tart, non-alcoholic
bar syrup

Martini

In a mixing glass filled with ice, combine:
2.5 ounces of gin
½ ounce of dry vermouth
Stir with a mixing spoon
Strain into a coupe or a martini glass or served on the rocks
Garnish with a lemon twist

Mary Pickford

In a shaker filled with ice, combine:
2 ounces of white rum
2 ounces of pineapple juice
¼ ounce Maraschino liqueur
¼ ounce grenadine
Shake and strain into a coupe or a martini glass
Garnish with brandy-soaked griotte cherries

Irish coffee

In a glass coffee mug, add a sugar cube and crush with a muddler
2 ounces of Irish whiskey
Fill ¾ of the remainder of the glass with hot coffee
Top with a dollop of unsweetened whip cream

Gin Rickey

In a mixing glass filled with ice, combine:
2 ounces of gin
¾ ounce fresh squeezed lime
Stir with a mixing spoon
Strain over fresh ice in a Collins glass
Top with sparkling water
Garnish with a lime wheel

Salud

Justin Razza is a bartender by trade and a Certified Sommelier. With an educational background in English, Education and Literature, he has been an editor and contributing writer for several publications and periodicals. When not behind a bar serving cocktails, you can usually find him seated at one imbibing and telling stories.
He lives in Charleston, South Carolina.

This is his first novel.

55056568R00107

Made in the USA
Columbia, SC
09 April 2019